Looking for Judah

Adventures in Genealogy and Remembrance

Stories of ancestry, place, and race

DAVID BRULE

Published by BookLocker.com, Inc., Bradenton, Florida.

Printed on acid-free paper.

This is a work of historical fiction, based on actual persons and events. The author has taken creative liberty with many details to enhance the reader's experience.

BookLocker.com, Inc.
2015

First Edition

Looking for Judah

"Adventures in genealogy and remembrance.
Stories of ancestry, place, and race"

Table of Contents

Foreword

"That this be empty tomb, or treasure, it depends on you. Do not enter, friend, without desire."

--Inscription at the entrance of the Museum of Mankind, Paris.

The story in these pages is a personal one, with strands of fact and fiction woven throughout, inspired by the imagery both real and spiritual of the Connecticut River Valley.

When we begin to investigate our origins, we never know what we will find. Some, of course don't care and never begin. For those others like myself, the search leads to unimagined discoveries, to new knowledge about your own self, to why you are in a given place, why you look the way you do, why you find familiarity and resonance within a landscape.

Of course, when investigating our genealogies and in trying to reconstruct what might have been the lives of our historical ancestors, we depend on a few facts gleaned from public records, and from anecdotal evidence preserved in family oral history and lore. Many of these sources, as well as all the others, may contain errors that belie the actual truth.

Therefore, it's quite likely that the stories contained in the following pages could have been written quite differently by others with similar family histories. There also could very well be multiple perspectives on the same evidence I've highlighted here, with someone else, a different writer, developing an entirely different scenario.

That said, your own search could lead to new acquaintances, to new discoveries and to a new understanding of our social and cultural history; it could quite possibly introduce a fascinating extended family.

You may well find, yet again, that family trees cross and re-cross, and can reveal astonishing interconnections.

For Betsy Strong, her children Judah, Sarah, Charles, and Solomon, as well as for the guiding hands of more than ten generations of ancestors, who have provided me with this story, and upon whose shoulders I stand.

Acknowledgements

This story would have been impossible to write without the exhaustive and diligent research of Barbara and Allen Ripingill. As is so evident throughout these pages, without our paths crossing at the opportune moment, the story would have remained buried and lost for all time. I owe them an unredeemable debt of gratitude.

Others who have contributed, inspired or encouraged the writing of this story include my cousin Donald Scott and our extended family, the Tatten and Jeffrey families of Nehantics, who along with Dr. John Pfeiffer of Lyme, have worked tirelessly to preserve the story of our Black Point Reservation ancestors.

Also, many thanks are extended to Richard Waterman of the East Lyme Historical Society, to Anne Marshall, Chris Grey, Nikki Barton and Tenzin of the Joseph Jeffrey house in Charlestown, Rhode Island, to Lynn Stowe Designs for exceptional graphic design support; to Dr. H. Martin Wobst, Chris Sawyer-Lauçanno, Jim and Felicity Callahan, Lyn Clark, Kelly Savage, author of the *Pond Dwellers,* and to Vickie Welch, author of *And They Were Related To....*

Why We Search

In each family there is one who seems called to find and remember the ancestors, to put flesh on their bones and make them live again, to tell the family story.

Genealogy is not the cold gathering of facts, but instead, it is an attempt to breathe life again into those who have gone before, and upon whose shoulders we stand.

We are the storytellers of the clan, the storytellers of the tribe. We have been called upon, as it were, by our elders who summon us to tell their story, so we do.

This task we are given goes beyond documenting facts. It goes to who we are and why we do the things we do. It goes to pride in what our ancestors were able to accomplish, how they contributed to what we are today. By telling their story, we pay respect to their hardships and losses, to their resoluteness and failings in the efforts to move forward. We try to understand the forces that made them choose to do what they did, and in choosing to do so, they made us who we are now.

Why do we keep looking? The search is never done. New information and new understandings are constantly coaxed out of hiding, out of memory buried deep in the past.

For some reason we are the ones who are meant to tell the story of our family. For some reason we feel the call to step up and restore the memory, to pass on the story, and to greet those whom we had never known before.

--Anonymous, and adapted by the author.

An Introduction, and an Explanation

Within these pages is found a family's history. The people and places depicted herein are real. No attempt has been made to change names or change the truth of the events. I hope the reader will receive this story in the spirit in which it was lived and written.

I have chosen an unusual chapter structure and sequence. Inspired by an earlier work by local writer Kelly Savage in *The Pond Dwellers*, I have chosen to have the elders, beginning with those 10 generations back, speak in their own voices before a family council, to teach the family lore and the family oral history, as would indigenous peoples all over the world. This is a timeless tradition and vehicle for learning that is sadly being lost in the present age, where families are more fragmented than ever before, when family gatherings become more and more rare.

The chapters alternate for the most part between two strands of the story: the first strand follows the unfolding contemporary adventures that kept us on the trail of the ancestors. The second strand leads through the life trajectories of key ancestors who each share their own stories, in their own words. Both strands are interwoven and culminate in the present.

This device of a weaving, alternating chapter sequence is the vehicle I have chosen to recount our modern genealogical adventure, while at the same time attempting to breathe life into the stories of those who have been long departed.

Hopefully the reader will be alert to the alternating time-frame, and understand the reasons. Both strands weave in and out, and converge at the end of this tale.

Prologue

River 1957

The long river has always been there.

We came to live on its banks in the house above the Narrows when I was not yet one year old, after the War.

The river is calm in the early morning. Mist wreaths rise up, the first of September on the Connecticut. Boat with boy and dog moves slowly through the Narrows. A dip of the oars from time to time encourages the old wooden rowboat to move through the fog. We drift between high red rock sides of the cleft in silence.

It's 8 AM, the oarlocks creak a bit, the dog in the bow shifts. Circles left behind on the surface by the dripping oars mark our path over the water. It's deep here, maybe over 140 feet, but we're headed for the shallows of the marsh on the other side, a little bit downriver.

Tribal people had known this place as Peskeompskut, the place where the river has split the rock. In the depths below us are sunken massive chains from 1910, used and abandoned by the log drivers to hold back the logs come down from the upper reaches. Farther below the ghost of chains is the deep hole of an ancient plunge pool formed more that 15,000 years before.

But as a twelve-year old sitting in a boat that morning, I wouldn't know that part of the story for another fifty years. Nor was there anyone to tell me that this river was going to be home for me. Drawn down to the shore from our snug house on the hill above, I followed the path to the edge as soon as I could prove that I could swim. There had been too many drowned in the river's history for parents to allow children to play on the banks. A treacherous drop-off a few feet out could lead you down through dark water to the abyss. It was scary and black in the waters but irresistible.

The river has a smell that is unmistakable, and it imprinted itself in me early. The smell of sand, mud, water against rock, fertile tropical valley where dinosaurs roamed, river flavored of pine, moss, fish, grasses and cattails. That in fact this river flowed through my veins and in the memory of my DNA, I would find out much, much later.

That foggy morning in the September silence was just one of the river's moods.

Winter often froze its surface two feet thick, the ice booming in the dark night, the river locked by the return of the glacier's ghost. That booming reached right into the bedrooms of the little house above. I waited there with visions of the fabled snow owl to come down the river of ice one of those frozen nights. Yellow fierce eyes, wisdom of the far north, hooting with the booming of the snowy-covered river.

In the early spring, the chaos of the break-up moved inexorably down, a wall of ice ramming straight into our shore, scraping the cattail marsh, grinding against the red rock, piling high in the débâcle, then side-slipping away in reluctance and anger from the immovable shore and roiling through the choking Narrows.

Summer brought people to the river, I didn't like that. My solitude and reveries were violated by the speeding boats, water skiers, the vulgarity of picnic trash, the penetrating splitting sound of the outboard motor. The river fluctuated then, drawn down by the mills to power their generators, that's when the mudflats were exposed. Sandpipers, plovers, and herons came to feed, and the shallow marshes became the Cape Cod of my mind, never having seen the real thing, never having been that far from home.

Autumn brought the ducks and geese from the north. In my imagination they carried with them the empty reaches of faraway places, the tundra, the taiga, the pine-scented wind wafting downstream.

Unlike other children, I took only a little of my time for baseball and bicycles, the river had me locked in its spell. I felt safe there. I could hide in the glades of ferns, in the tangle of vines, in the cattails if need be, all night long, or so I imagined. I was at home with river mud on my feet, legs, and arms. The river was in my nostrils and lungs, sun reflected from its surface burned into my face, into my mind, my heart swelled with the rank scent, its presence quieted my young spirit, gave me assurance and steadiness.

Integrated with the river, I later was to carry this spirit within me to places far away from my homeland banks.

I was beginning a long and unconscious apprenticeship; I didn't know it at that time. Something ancient was awakening in me. Some benign presence was speaking to me through the murmurings in the stone and the flowing water. I was learning to use the gift of seeing with quiet eyes.

Because of this time, I would come to be at ease with multiple identities, to go between multiple worlds.

Because of this time, I would come to learn that being here in this place was no accident.

Chapter 1

The Portrait in the Den 1973

It all seemed to begin on a hot August afternoon in 1973. I found myself in a quiet home on Pleasant Street. The home belonged to granduncle Douglas Smith. The kitchen was spotless, the den still faintly smelled of cigar smoke. Shelves were lined with baseball mementos, for Uncle Doug was something of a celebrity in these parts.

A baseball phenomenon when he and the sport were young, he had gone from high school and the family farm to playing in the new Fenway Park in 1912, as a relief pitcher for the World Series-bound Boston Red Sox. He didn't make the Series team, having been shipped out to the Minors at season's end. He was to spend a decade pitching up and down the Eastern seaboard before retiring from the game. He had lived out his life in this house, in a quiet residential neighborhood, not a mile from the homestead where he was born. And now we had the task of going through his things.

When his legs finally gave out at the age of eighty-three, it was time for the retirement home, though his mind was still sharp. Since he had no children, it fell to us to get him to a safe place for his final days. We had wheeled him up the walk to the rest home and another old timer taking the sun on the veranda had recognized him and had called out to him. Doug's face had beamed at that, and the winning smile of the old days flashed over him as he touched his cap just as he would have when he walked off the field after one of his victories.

So now there we were, in the immaculate home, looking just as he had left it days before. The clock still ticked on the mantelpiece, old photographs of his dogs still guarded his den.

Pete and I were getting ready to start removing his effects prior to selling the place, for it was sure that he'd not be back. Pete, by the way, was actually my aunt. Her real name was Elizabeth, a name which I was to discover in later years was part of the naming pattern in family lore. A lovely name, but few in the family by that name were blessed with good fortune, as I was also destined to discover.

Now, how Aunt Pete came by her boy's nickname, no one knows for sure. One likely possibility for the nickname was that her parents were hoping their first-born would be a boy. Regardless of gender, fairly soon she was expected to take on all the farm chores as would an eldest son. I'd say that formed her character, because she became a no-nonsense, tough customer. She was as feisty as anyone in this family, the heaviest smoker, the best at swearing and cursing, she could hold her whiskey and drink any challenger under the table. Besides being able to cuss and drink with the best of them, she was my godmother, which meant something in those days.

So a bond between us had formed early on. She was also the keeper of the family oral history, the only one of her generation with the inquisitive mind and interest to listen and to remember the stories of the old people of the family who came before us. And that linked the two of us together forever.

That day in August we made our way through a lifetime of Douglas's accumulated belongings. Luckily he was one of those who saved everything and kept his souvenirs in mint condition. There were letters from the Great War, baseball clippings, post cards and calling cards, photographs of forgotten men in top hats and straw boaters, pictures of lovely women with impossibly narrow waists, ungainly hats and ample bosoms.

A year or two earlier, in this very den, an old man had sat primly in the now empty wooden rocker. The left arm that fired the most feared fastball in this part of the state rested quietly, holding a cigar that he raised once in a while to make a point as he re-told his old stories to the reporter who had come up the walk to pay a call. Doug's feet in old fashioned high top lace-up shoes, remained side by side barely moving as he rocked.

He traveled back in time once again that day to the turn of the century when, luckily for him, he discovered early that he loved the game of baseball, and that no one could hit his blazing pitches.

He went from playing ball in the pasture below the barn to pitching for town teams, unbeatable with his brothers making up most of the infield. My grandfather Alan, nicknamed Abe, was his catcher, brother Clint was third baseman, brother Butch played second, and oldest brother Billy was manager.

By the time he reached high school he was striking out upwards of twenty batters a game. He chuckled in his rocking chair, remembering how his mother Elizabeth, a stern Scottish Calvinist from Aberdeen, tolerated no breaking of the Sabbath, keeping all family members sitting quietly in the kitchen on a Sunday reading the Bible, with nothing to break the silence except the ticking of the clock of a hot summer day. She did make an exception however, for her darling Doug, who was allowed to go outside to practice with Abe. He pitched hard, burning the ball into his brother's mitt, the regular whoosh and thwack resounding time after time.

It wasn't long before the Red Sox came around looking at this prospect. They liked what they saw, and brought him right out of high school to the new Fenway Park as a relief pitcher, in July of 1912. He worked three innings and did a good job, as he liked to tell it, but the Sox had so much power in those days, with the likes of teammates Tris Speaker, Harry Hooper, Duffy

Lewis and Smokey Joe Wood, that Doug was shipped out to a farm team right after his first game, and before the World Series.

He never got back to Fenway. His eyes always darkened when he reached that part of the story. He had been released by the Sox suddenly in 1913. The Boston papers reported that it was because of a "bad heart." He never told us the real story, and I wouldn't find it out until years later. Needless to say he and his brothers became die-hard Yankees fans, always rooting for those arch-enemies of the Red Sox, and somewhat of a contradiction and a rarity in this part of Massachusetts.

Now he was miles away in a rest home, far from his beloved house on Pleasant Street, beginning the last few weeks of his long life.

Pete and I went back to boxing up the belongings, each quiet and lost in our own thoughts. The venitian blinds had been drawn almost closed against the August heat, giving the dark interior a semblance of coolness. Through the motes floating in a beam of sunlight that had filtered in, I first saw it.

There it was: a family portrait in a neat dark oak frame. The group posed, frozen in time, looking directly at the camera. At first I recognized no one in the photograph, although bit by bit as the faces came into focus, I recognized the familiar over-sized ears of my grandfather Abe. But he was only ten years old in the picture.

My gaze moved to the man sitting sternly next to his wife. Massive hands, high cheekbones, sharp goatee, something about his eyes. He had a straight-backed self-satisfied look, with his wife and five sons arranged for the camera. I had never seen this portrait before. Pete caught me staring at the old gent in the picture.

"That's Judah" says Pete. "He's your great-grandfather"

4

I kept staring. Judah and I had never set eyes on one another before this. He was the man who, in 1882, had bought the homestead along the river that I was now living in. He was the one who had founded the family, and yet I had never seen an image of him before, even though I now lived in his house. His eyes locked on mine, aloof as if challenging me to try to figure him out, to penetrate the enigma he was about to pose.

"He was...*different.*" says Pete. She went on:

"This is the story I got from my grandmother Elizabeth, that's her next to Judah. But what I'm going to say, you can't tell anybody ever. I'd get in trouble with the whole family. They made us all promise never to tell. And now you've got to promise too. But I can't go to my grave and have the story be lost about where we come from."

My eyes widened as she revealed the family secret buried since Judah's death in 1929, when the conspiracy of family silence began. And I never did tell anybody for more than thirty years, even after Pete's death, that is until about a year ago, when things started falling into place.

Chapter 2

Joseph Jeffrey (1695-1780)

Remember this:
Time is not a straight line between then and now. Time flows forward, and it can flow back, it can coil about in spirals, and come around again.

...Those who no longer walk among the living are still considered living, but in the spirit world. Those worlds are not completely separate.
Indigenous beliefs

It is mid August.
Inside the house, a crackling fire in the stone fireplace. In spite of the season, it is needed to keep the dank air from the room. The mill pond outside the west window shimmers in the dusk. Drumbeats from the Narragansett Gathering are carried on the evening air reaching even into the room where we are assembled.

It is to be a long night of remembrance and story-telling. Tobacco smoke and sweetgrass smoke mingle. Some shadows already dance on the age-darkened wood paneling on the wall. The low colonial ceiling carries the smoke, the shadows, and 300 years of time. We wait.

We have all traveled back to the ancestral home, the house of Joseph Jeffrey on the Narragansett Reservation in Rhode Island. This will be the first of many visits to hear the stories of our family's beginnings, to be told by the ancestors, by those who came before us. All of us in the room are blood relatives, representing the ten generations of family, connected back through the ages. Many seated with us are already in the spirit world.

We are waiting for the man who built this house, our ancestor, to speak. He has called us here, and we wait. We gaze silently into the flames.

Soon he appears, emerging from the shadows near the wall. He moves to the family circle, stands in front of the hearth. He is tall, dignified, skin the color of mahogany, black hair cropped in the colonial fashion. He's wearing a rough-spun cotton shirt, a black waistcoat, long buckskin leggings, moccasins. He looks at each of us for long minutes, and then speaks:

"I am Joseph Jeffrey. I am proud that you are gathered here in my house, this house I built with my own hands for myself and my children, in 1720. I am showing myself to you because it is the right time for you to hear me, you are ready, and have come here to finally meet me. I am proud to see you, my descendants unto even my 7th great-grandsons, ten generations of my blood line. There are those among you who were and will be leaders, others of you are the keepers of the fire, carrying its light and with it, our knowledge. Some of you are warriors, some of you are peacemakers. Many of you have become Go-betweens. It is good that you are here. Our family story will not be lost now.

I was born not far from here in 1695 in our summer *wetu*. My father was away, gone as far as the valley of the great blue river, the Quinneticook, scouting with the English, hunting and fishing in Pocumtuk and Peskeompskut. I am Nehantic and Narragansett, and I sat on the Sachem's Council.

Before I was born, the great Ninigret the Elder guided us and kept us from harm by the English. We saw what they had done to the Pequot, and although we feared and disliked the Pequot, we learned how cruel and merciless the English could be. My cousins the Montauk had survived by allying with the white men. They did not suffer as the Wampanoag, the Nipmuk, and the Narragansett would, by the hands of the English. Ninigret told us that we should become similar to the English, for he had seen in a vision that they would grow in strength and power and never leave this land. We changed our given tribal names, we left the Indian spirit ways for the Anglican beliefs. We attended church, we listened to their preachers, although we disapproved that they did not use their own words. Instead they stole words from their ancient prophets in their book called the Bible. We thought them weak for this, but we did not protest. Later, some did. They gave one of our preachers, Joseph Fish, some very difficult years by and by.

We saw what the English did to Metacomet, to Canonchet, to the other Narragansetts who dared defy them. We saw the Great Swamp Massacre not far from here, where some Jeffreys died. We saw the slaughter of old men, women, and children at Peskeompskut. We adopted English ways because we knew they would destroy us if we did not.

By embracing the white man's ways, we hoped to survive. From them, I learned the carpenter's trade and the sawyer's trade. Ninigret the Younger, Ninigret II , became Sachem in 1692, years after the Nehantics had taken in survivors of the Pequot and Narragansett people to protect them. He was Sachem when the reservation was established in 1708. Ninigret granted me this site and I built my house and sawmill here where we are now gathered. The house is bigger now, but still sturdy. I built well and lived in safety here.

But that was not to last. Shortly after my first son George was born in 1718, Ninigret died and many others of the royal bloodline of the Ninigrets succeeded him down through the years. I was part of the Sachem's Council because of my noble lineage, I was advisor to the Ninigrets during those years. But when Thomas Ninigret succeeded Charles, and then George Ninigret, in 1745, my troubles began.

Tom did not always act wisely as protector of his lands and people, and very soon the tribe began to pull apart from inside. Many disapproved of Tom, for he had a weakness for strong drink and playing games of chance, which he continually lost to white men. Some of the tribe were angered when he gave away land and timber to pay back his debts. Many who fought against Tom, also did not approve of the Anglican minister and sought Separate Ways to worship, ways similar to the old Indian beliefs. These times were painful for our family. Many of my children returned to our ancient Nehantic lands at the mouth of the Quinneticook in what is now called Black Point in Lyme. My grandchildren were born there, and many of them were never to set eyes upon their grandfather.

King Tom's troubles grew. He gave up more and more land, including this house. I had to leave, and I had great sorrow in doing that. I knew that my best days were done. But I did not give up.

After Tom's death in 1769, I fought in the English courts to get my house and sawmill back. But bit by bit it was clear that the whites who coveted our lands on the reservation were finding ways to take it over. I moved away to other parts, but kept coming back here to see if I could stay and die in my own place. But most of my children had left, gone to the Nehantic lands of the forefathers at the mouth of the great river.

I will not tell you where my body lies. It is not even familiar to me. But my heart is here, and my heart is joyful now in the spirit world. I have come here to see you gathered, so that you would see and hear me together. My hand has guided many of you in your life's journeys before. You may have felt that, but you could not know that, if your heart was not open. I am here. You may call on me if you need me."

His eyes burned as he looked again at each of us. He stepped away from the light, to the back of the chamber and blended with the smoke of the tobacco and the sweetgrass.

Chapter 3

Two Windsors 2006

It was the last Sunday afternoon before Christmas, 2006. The first knock and clamor at the door began the renewal of the generations-old tradition of pulling the extended family back to the homestead Judah and his wife Lizzie bought back in 1882. With that first knock the flow started: in came cousins Tom and Joan, with their grandchildren visiting from California. Right after him, and in short order the house filled up with aunts, uncles, cousins, sisters, brothers, in-laws, stepchildren, and grandparents all under one roof again for a short while.

The dog lifts his wizened old head briefly, figuring that was the end of his plans for a quiet Sunday snooze next to the woodstove. That 1912 Glenwood C cookstove is fired up and heaped with potluck dishes, the kitchen table is piled with desserts, wines and whiskeys. The excited talk and Christmas greetings fill the house to the rafters, rising up to the spirit world high in the attic. Adventures, jokes, mishaps are shared and repeated round the rooms of the house as the noise level rises. The generations mix, the children romp with the new toys and with the cousins they rarely see but once a year, the adults get caught up with the past few months' news. The octogenarians of the family are back together in the ancestral home, and spend hours visiting just out of the maelstrom swirling around the room.

At one point, I brought the youngest of the family, the rare visitors from the west coast, face-to-face with the portrait I had brought from that den back in 1973. I had kept Pete's secret as I had promised, but it didn't keep me from putting Judah, Lizzie and their family back where they belonged, on their own parlor wall. So there was Judah again, looking sternly and confidently out at them from the 1880s. The children stared at their great-great-great grandparents, who had actually lived, and died, in these rooms. The meeting was the children's beginning of a connection to this house and land, and that was the main point of the family gathering: to renew a sense of place.

Before long, the children headed out to the woods along the river like all the children down the one hundred and twenty-five years of our family before them. Happy to escape the confines of the house and the adults, they were off to skim stones on the quiet river, their joyful shouts and laughter echoing and ringing through the valley.

During a quiet moment in the festive mayhem, Paula, a cousin from far-away California, and I found ourselves together in the parlor, in front of the fireplace hearth. I knew through the grapevine that she was interested in family lore, and had begun, with her mother's help, researching the family genealogy. My pulse quickened, maybe just maybe, this was a kindred spirit. Since she rarely visited our ancestral home, I might only have this one chance to share some of the oral history I had gleaned from living in this house and in this village, where our family has had such a long history. Perhaps I could finally share the secret with someone. The secret that I had promised not to divulge, a promise to Pete made more that thirty years ago in that den of a then dying and now long dead granduncle. Over the years I had carefully gathered various photographs of great grandmother Lizzie, her five sons at different periods of their lives, and her imposing husband Judah. I carefully shared the photographs, one by one, with my cousin. Still I held the secret back, but the blood was pounding in my ears.

"See him, your great-great grandfather Judah?" I said to Paula. I was still hesitant. Should I come right out with it? I found myself searching for some of Aunt Pete's cautious words from 1973, that August afternoon in the den. "He was *different.*"

I began a roundabout story, still struggling inside with how much I should say. I told my cousin that on various birth certificates and death certificates in the town hall, Judah's birthplace had sometimes been written as Windsor, Vermont, and sometimes Windsor, Connecticut. When I read those records, in the old penmanship of the 1880s, the abbreviations "Vt." sometimes look like "Ct." and vice versa. No doubt about the Windsor part, though. I had already journeyed to Windsor, Vermont to look up birth records in person. Curiously, the town clerk was the aunt of a teacher I had hired two years before to teach Spanish in my high school language department. I was learning to read signs and not just dismiss as coincidence what could appear to be random chance. The adage that things happen for a reason was going to prove true all through this story of Judah.

What hand was guiding me through this search? I figured that if any teacher I had hired happened to have an aunt in Windsor, Vermont, that meant I was supposed to go there to look for my great grandfather. I did go, and I found... nothing. No Judah Smith in the years between 1850 and 1860, not before nor after. Nothing.

I turned to my cousin, and pointed to Judah in another photograph, sitting high up on the seat of his delivery wagon, Old Dan his horse standing proudly, both posing for the Howes Brothers photo. I was about to repeat... "There's something *different* about him..." when the flow of the party drifted back to surround us, with laughing and rollicking children, and adults intent on telling their latest jokes. I didn't continue our conversation.

That night, Paula called from her mother's home. Her mother, Barbara, had recently moved back from California, here to her home town. She was about to become a close collaborator and friend, although neither of us could guess at that moment how important that first phone call was to be. She was a genealogist with a keen interest in history, she was working on the story of our interconnected families, and, although neither of us realized it at the time, she was going to lead the developing quest to find Judah.

I told her what I knew about him, and the two Windsors, but not Pete's secret. I told her of the dead end in Windsor, Vermont. No Judah up there. Then it was her turn. She told me that in her search of genealogy records through *ancestry.com* and all, that she was only able to find *one* Judah Smith, he was from Windsor alright, but in Connecticut. She was sure it couldn't be our Judah because he was listed as a Free Person of Color, on some censuses, as "mulatto" on others, his siblings were black.

"Well, Barbara" I said, breaking my thirty year promise to Pete.

"I have to tell you something."

Chapter 4

Rebecca Jeffrey (1781-1850)

We are waiting quietly in front of the fire, still in Joseph Jeffrey's Rhode Island house. The dusk has now settled on the mill pond outside the window. Flames flicker on faces, on walls behind. Joseph has spoken, and left us there. The room remains quiet, each of us lost in thought. I have heard of the custom of the Talking Stick for the one who wishes to speak. There is none. It would be better if we got one, next time. Pine crackles in the fire, sparks rise up the ancient throat of the chimney. The heartbeat of the Narragansett drumming still sounds, low, constant, distant.

A woman steps forward, she is carrying a Talking Stick in her right hand. She stands before the fire, warming, and facing us. She is tall and dignified, a dark blue dress reaches the floor; the collar rises up tight under her chin. A bright red shawl is draped about her; jet- black hair, braided in a single tress, hangs to her waist over her right shoulder. Her nose is straight and well-formed, her mouth firm, her eyes dark. Glints of humor are hidden in the corners of her features... She speaks:

"I am Rebecca Jeffrey. I am pleased to be in my great-grandfather's house again. I am pleased to see you have come here to meet me, and that you heard our call to you to come home again. Those of you, even our great-grand children's children have heard us and have come to renew our proud history. It is high time. We do not want our story forgotten. We do not want our story twisted.

I am an ancient one. I was born in 1781. My life began in Lyme, on Nehantic tribal lands on Black Point. My father was

George Jeffrey the younger, son of my grandfather who was also named George Jeffrey, son of Joseph. Grandfather was born near here, before this house was built, by his father. He was born on these Nehantic and Narragansett lands in 1718.

We Nehantics moved about with the seasons, as did all tribes near us: the Pequots, Mohegans, Narragansetts. We are all related, one way or another, through marriage or blood.

My grandfather George moved away from here back to Nehantic Reserve lands in the 1730s. It was best for us to live in our own towns, in Lyme, East Haddam, and Black Point. My father was born in Lyme in 1750, he married my mother Sarah there in 1779, and he had many children, besides me. I remember now my brother Joseph, named for great-grandfather, my brother Asa, my sisters Abigail and Huldah. There may have been others, but I don't remember them all, at my age.

At least three times a year we moved on the paths of the ancestors, and came back to the Narragansett church on this reservation, especially for this August Gathering, just as you have come here now.

This is where we always met our cousins the Montauk, the Pequot, the Narragansett. Even the Mohegans came, some of their past treacheries now avenged, but it would be a long time before true peace was settled between us. It was probably best that our family no longer lived here though. There were too many jealousies and bad feelings lingering over Tom Ninigret, the Anglican minister Joseph Fish, and the Anti-Sachem Party. The families who did not trust Tom the Sachem any longer had hard feelings against us, since we had always been a part of the Ninigret family's Council. I must admit, they may have had reason, because Tom created many problems for the tribe.

Back in Connecticut we lived on our lands on Black Point in Lyme during the summer, and in the winter we moved further inland to the Gungy tract, where my father and his father had tribal claim to hunt, harvest wood, and winter over there. Even then, we were constantly pressed by the whites who wanted more and more land, who used their land badly, and never had enough.

We had by then understood the meaning of their sickness for fencing in their lands. Too bad many of the Nehantics were willing to sell, even though it was against our custom. How can you sell land that you do not own? But we had debts, we wanted English goods, and our Nehantic population was dropping, with so many seeking work off the reserve. So there were few left to complain. Many of us left our tribal lands to work in cities or to find land to farm. Some of us from the tribe just leased tribal lands to the English and held a mortgage on that land. We expected to reclaim it one day, but sometimes after many years had passed, the whites felt they had paid enough and that they had ownership. We lost land there piece by piece.

Many Nehantic felt they needed to get entirely away from the land-hungry whites. They followed the Mohegan leader Samson Occum to Brothertown in Oneida country in New York where the Iroquois nation gave sanctuary to all tribes from here who wished to move away from the Europeans. My brother Asa went there. I stayed in Lyme and East Haddam, it was what I was meant to do.

In 1798, I decided to marry William Mason. I will tell you, I knew right off when I first saw him that he would be a good mate. His father was Cooley Mason, born in Branford in 1754. One of Cooley's wives was Clorinda Robbins. He married her in 1781. My husband William, son of Clorinda, was born in East Haddam. His descendants still live there.

He was a handsome man, tall and strong, and we lived well in Lyme. When my father George died he left us some money and some land. We were able to use that to keep William's business of building wagons and wheels going.

Just the same, we felt the ways of our fathers slipping away, along with the lands. By the time we were married in 1798, there were hardly more than thirty people left living on the Nehantic reservation at Black Point.

Later, the ones left on Black Point accepted to sell the last tribal lands, but retained tribal claims to the Nehantic burial ground there, which the Town of Lyme accepted to protect in perpetuity. Even though we were heart-broken to sell our last land, we knew that at least the ancestors would dwell in peace in their cemetery lands forever.

Many Nehantics were gone to Brothertown, many lived in towns, many married outside the tribe, to whites or blacks. The officials started calling us "Free People of Color". I didn't mind so much, for we had always been free, never slaves, at least in the Jeffrey family. They began calling us "mulattos" too. They used all those other terms so they wouldn't have to call us Indians. We were baptized as Indian in the church in Lyme, but they started calling us other names, because they wanted our lands. If they didn't count Indians, then Indians didn't exist. With those other names, we were becoming invisible to them.

Many of us Jeffreys did not put up with their ways of making us invisible. Asa, his children, and descendants got involved with groups to help us keep our churches, to bring back our kinsmen who were taken away. My own father helped Cuff Condol get his freedom back in 1787. My brother Joseph married Cuff's daughter Melinda, and later helped emancipate Herod Brooks in 1814. He bought him back from slavery in that year. Later Herod married my sister Abigail. That was one way to get a husband!

William and I had five children, Rebecca, George, Eunice, Judith, and Amos. Judith was born in Lyme in 1800; she was destined to move up to Deerfield with her husband John Mason Strong, her children and grandchildren. She is here with you now, with us. John Mason Strong was one of William's kinsmen. In the 1870s, they moved up the river to Deerfield and lived out their lives in that valley. By the 1830s, we too moved up the river to Hartford with Amos. We lived in a nice frame house until the end. Amos took good care of us in those last years between 1830 and 1850.

So, as I said, the Nehantics who stayed in Lyme agreed to sell the last tribal farm lands, but not that sacred place, our cemetery at Black Point, where the ancestors' bones are lying. Those people still living on the reserve needed to get some money to finish their days. It was a very sad time. But I have joy in my heart for I know that some of you here will go back to Black Point to remember, to pray, and to sing over the graves of our fathers and mothers. I ask you to do that. They will rejoice when you return to find them.

But we Nehantics are still here, I can see our people in you that have come this day to Joseph's house. We Jeffreys, we Nehantics are still here, in you. That is a great comfort to me.

I'll leave you now. I've said what I wanted to say to you. Now I know our story will not be lost. But one more thing I want you to remember: all of you here come from the First People. We have the noble, warrior bloodlines of the Nehantic, Montauk, Pequot, and Narragansett. We have worked with Frederick Douglass, fought in the Massachusetts Glory Regiment, helped Susan B. Anthony, Reverend Beman and many others, to help our people, to be of service to others. We have always been Free People.

You are here because you came after us, but you are of us. You will remain strong. You will be proud. You will stand tall, it is your lineage, you will carry the honor of your ancestors."

She stood fierce and erect. Her eyes blazed, then softened. Her defiant mouth curved in a hint of a smile.

After she had moved back into the shadows, we saw the Talking Stick she had left, leaning against the fireplace stones. A bright ribbon on it held the strong feathers of the red-tailed hawk, the delicate red feathers of the cardinal, brilliant blue of the jay and the yellow shaft of the flicker. They shifted slightly in the glow of the fire light.

Joseph Jeffrey – Judith M. Mason

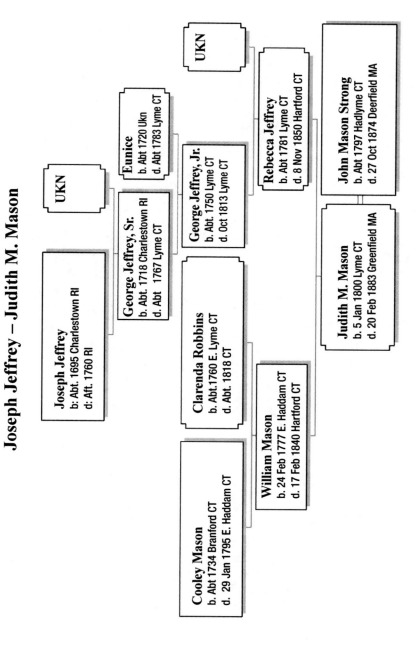

UKN

Joseph Jeffrey
b: Abt. 1695 Charlestown RI
d: Aft. 1760 RI

UKN

Eunice
b: Abt 1720 Ukn
d: Abt 1783 Lyme CT

George Jeffrey, Sr.
b: Abt. 1718 Charlestown RI
d: Abt 1767 Lyme CT

George Jeffrey, Jr.
b: Abt. 1750 Lyme CT
d: Oct 1813 Lyme CT

Clarenda Robbins
b: Abt.1760 E. Lyme CT
d: Abt. 1818 CT

Rebecca Jeffrey
b: Abt 1781 Lyme CT
d: 8 Nov 1850 Hartford CT

Cooley Mason
b: Abt 1734 Branford CT
d: 29 Jan 1795 E. Haddam CT

William Mason
b: 24 Feb 1777 E. Haddam CT
d: 17 Feb 1840 Hartford CT

John Mason Strong
b: Abt 1797 Hadlyme CT
d: 27 Oct 1874 Deerfield MA

Judith M. Mason
b: 5 Jan 1800 Lyme CT
d: 20 Feb 1883 Greenfield MA

Chapter 5

The Door Open Again

The next several months of 2007 went by in a blur. Life's obligations kept us busy, and the search to find Judah stayed on the back burner. Just the same, echoes reached cousins throughout the extended family that Barbara had cracked the case wide open. But we had to wait while the family tree was slowly being traced back through all the branches. Barbara wanted to get it absolutely right before sharing something perhaps not totally accurate. By May we couldn't wait any longer, and I broke the ice by calling Barbara to find out what she had discovered.

"You'd better sit down" she said business-like. "Have you got paper and pen ready? Here goes."

My heart was pounding as she started tracing Judah from the time he settled in Millers Falls, back through his history that had been kept behind closed doors for three generations. I was about to hear a litany of ancestral family names that were to become achingly familiar from this point on.

She had traced the Judah William Smith of Windsor, *Connecticut* to his parents. Judah was born in 1853, as was marked on his tombstone in the cemetery not far from this homestead where we are now living. His father's name was William Smith (hence Judah's middle name) and his mother was…*Betsy Strong.* I had never heard that name before, at least not in family lore. I had seen William's name on Judah's death certificate in the Town Hall, but his mother was not named. In fact, the notation on the document was that the name of his mother "*cannot be known.*"

(Much later we found Judah's marriage certificate listing Betsy as his mother and as having attended the wedding ceremony. Surely Judah's wife Lizzie should have remembered that!)

"Now," said Barbara. I held my breath. "Betsy was born in 1839, which means she had Judah when she was fourteen years old."

Fourteen years old! What drama, scandal, or crime could have been behind that?

Barbara went on: she had found that a William Smith was mentioned in one census as a boatman on the Connecticut River, but other than that, there was no record of his existence anywhere else. So, apparently this William Smith disappeared from the scene almost immediately, which was certainly suspicious. And yet, by piecing together the naming patterns in the family, Judah's middle name was William, he named his first son William, born in 1881, and William continued to be on all the pertinent certificates. But why had Betsy Strong's name disappeared from family memory in less than 100 years? Judah had died in 1929, and surely among his children, someone would have remembered the name of their grandmother who had lived in Deerfield, less than six miles away.

Even Pete, who knew as much as was knowable about the family, having learned some of the story from her stern tight-lipped grandmother Lizzie , Judah's wife, never mentioned Betsy. Why no Betsy Strong?

"Well," said Barbara, "Betsy had three other children besides Judah."

So Great grandfather had siblings, and why shouldn't he?

"She had a daughter two years after Judah, and her name was Sarah Sharpe."

It seems Betsy had had a second child by a different man, Elijah William Sharpe.

"By 1870," Barbara continued, "Betsy had married one Charles H. Scott and had two more children, Solomon and Charles II."

This was getting complicated, but it's what I wanted to know.

"Now , the next part is interesting: in the various censuses I've checked, going back to 1860, Betsy, Judah, and his siblings are listed as...Free People of Color. At other times, they're called mulatto."

My head was spinning, my pulse was off the charts. Feelings of confusion, wonder, joy, and pride washed over me. What was that supposed to mean: "Mulatto, Free Person of Color?"

The first term I had heard, never thinking it could apply to my own family, the second term had never entered any frame of reference of mine. From then on however, these terms would become very familiar; they would begin redefining me, redefining who I was, or shedding new light on a part of my heritage.

I began to understand that someone had not wanted me to find this out.

The phone call lasted an hour, and revelation after revelation came forward. But what left me stunned once again, was the fact that my Betsy Strong, Judah's mother, was buried in the Deerfield cemetery, with her daughter Sarah, her daughter's husband William Barnes, and their five sons. Betsy and her family, including Judah, had moved steadily up the Connecticut River, *my* Connecticut River from New Haven, to Wallingford, to Hartford, to Windsor, and Deerfield. By the mid 1870s, all were living and farming in Deerfield, including Judah's grandparents John Mason Strong and Judith Mason, whose married name thus became Judith Mason Strong. All of a sudden, my family tree revealed hidden branches, and extended family names were popping out all over: Smith, Strong, Mason, and Scott.

Once one door opens, it leads to another and another. I was soon to come face to face with another branch of the family, lost to us sometime after 1920, and in some eyes, with good reason.

Later in the month, a chance phone call led to the next revelation, and a vital link to one of Judah's siblings. One morning, at Barbara's home, the phone rang. A certain Donald Scott was on the line. A Thirty-three Degree Mason, from one town away, he was speaking to Allen, Barbara's husband. They were arranging Donald's sponsorship of Allen into the Lodge, when Barbara's ears perked up.

"*Donald Scott?*" she queried. "Ask him if his mother's name was Bernice!" she called out, rapidly scanning the Smith/Strong/Scott family tree always at the ready on her computer.

"He says yes," responded Allen.

"Ask him if his father's name was Solomon!" Barbara was hot on a fresh trail.

"He says, why *yes!*" called out Allen."

"Ask him if his grandfather was Charles H. Scott! Was his great-grandmother Betsy Strong?"

A hearty booming laugh came out over the phone.

"How on earth does she know *that?*" the deep unmistakable baritone of an African-American man could be heard coming over the phone.

"Well" replied Allen. "Barbara thinks our family trees crossed, a few generations back."

That door long closed between Judah and his siblings began to crack open, with light now leaking into a room long kept dark by a family secret and a conspiracy of silence. That light was bringing me face to face with the pathological, persistent trauma of racial prejudice in America.

Chapter 6

To Honor the Fiddler 2007

"Everything happens for a reason"
—American Zen folk saying

Like following a thread through a labyrinth, we move from one chamber to the next, always finding another door at the far end. Passing through, another extraordinary circumstance leads us into the past, only to help explain the present.

What started with an unfortunate series of events in the early fall of 2007 led us further into the maze, but from these events came new discoveries.

We had recently helped Mamadou, an African colleague from Gambia, move into his newly rented house in the next town over from us, barely five miles away. Within a few days, racist epithets were scrawled in chalk around the neighborhood and on his driveway. Our friend already had experiences with this type of small-town racism. He was feisty, and determined. He was not going to let this pass. He contacted the authorities who conducted an investigation that reached no specific conclusions. Surely however, a small friendly town would find an appropriate reaction. In another twist of fate, in a story full of such twists, this incident set a series of events in motion that would lead me face to face with the family I had lost.

The local cultural council decided to take action to attempt to bring back into perspective the multiracial history of the town. They came upon the idea of heightening the visibility of an annual event in the fall of the year, the Fiddlers' Gathering. For several years prior, musicians had been coming together in the town park to honor a well-known local fiddler and contra-dance caller from the 1870s, John Putnam. John had been quite unique. Not only did he play his fiddle left-handed, and call contra dances throughout the region, (a New England tradition dating back to pre-revolutionary times), but also, he was a barber, an important figure in the Underground Railroad, and he was black.

To raise awareness of this low-profile meeting of musicians, the council decided to create an unusual happening as an answer to the racist incident involving our friend. They would locate Putnam's grave in the colored section of the Green River Cemetery, they would provide a tombstone for him and his wife, and they would put out a call to all his relatives scattered far and wide, to come home for the placing of the tombstone and for a reunion of Putnam's extended family.

My cousin Barbara, who had been working diligently on all the branches of our own family, read about the event in the local newspaper. She saw a golden opportunity and said,

"We've got to get over there. I have a feeling you're going to meet your family."

So on that wet Saturday morning we headed for the next town, through Cheapside on the banks of the Connecticut, up Deerfield Street, bound for the Green River Cemetery. (Again, much later, I was to discover that I had followed that day a route that Judah and his siblings had taken many times in their lives. Unknowingly, I even passed by the place where they used to live!)

We made our way through the graves to the part of the cemetery where the colored folks of past generations were buried. In the cool, wet, and grey air of the morning, the distant sounds of hymns and spirituals drifted up from among the worn, lichen-covered tombstones. Eighty or so people were gathered under the trees to celebrate, at long-last, the placing of the stone to honor the memory of John Putnam and his wife. Putnam's great- great -granddaughter Juanita H. and her own daughter Christine lent their rich textured voices to the ethereal light quality of the Amandla Chorus. Rodney Miller and Susan Conger, fiddlers from a nearby town, had been invited to play there at the grave, to evoke for a short time the sound of that distant fiddle, to give a tangible sense in peoples' minds of the jubilation of dancers, balancing and swinging, ephemeral couples set to *dos à dos* and promenade in the brightening morning air.

We stood there off to the side with our friend Mamadou who had been the object of the racist remarks, and who was one of the catalysts of this event. I looked over the extended family arrayed before the grave for the reunion photo: every shade of skin possible, from rich African texture to mahogany to café-crème with freckles to white. I was new at this. *Where* did I fit in? *Did* I fit in? Maybe I shouldn't even bring it up.

Beyond the remembrance and the festivity of the communal music, I was looking for something more intangible, trying to conjure up some feel in the air for my own ancestor.

Perhaps the clues were written in the tombstones. The new one over John Putnam, and a much older one in Millers Falls, over my great grandfather Judah. He himself was a fiddler, and also a contemporary of John Putnam. The span of their lives, their trajectories had crossed, back in the 1870s.

John was getting to be an old man by then when, in those years, he and Judah lived in the same neighborhood for a short while. Knowing that those who were then called Colored tended to live together on the same margins of white society, I had the growing suspicion that he and Judah were part of that same community. I'd like to think that they knew each other, this being a small town and colored people few at the time, and that maybe even John taught Judah a few things on the fiddle. Judah was a young man then, about to be married and to move to the farm on the river where we now live.

Judah's sister Sarah had married shortly after his move to the next town, and because of her dark skin became defined as black. We later learned that she did marry a white man, William Barnes, but her children considered themselves black, and they married into the black community, while Judah moved off to pass for white. Sarah had five sons who married into the African American community, and most of their descendants married into the families now present at Putnam's reunion. My great aunt's granddaughter had even married a grandson of John Putnam himself! I was coming to realize that I was probably related to most of the families gathered there at the gravesite, either by blood or by marriage. Yet I could tell no one.

But my friend Mamadou knew of the secret, and he was having a hard time controlling bursts of laughter that were welling up inside him. My quandary amused him, and I'm sure my disorientation showed, although he was the only one to grasp the humor of the situation.

A prominent black politician, a successful lawyer, and a descendant of Putnam, began a brief speech. At one point he said:

"Well, it's moving to see so many friends, musicians and family gathered here to honor Ol' Put'. Of course, you can tell just by looking at us, who his relatives are."

Mamadou's stifled mirth was getting contagious. I whispered out of the corner of my mouth to him,

"Brother, you don't know the half of it!" Mamadou slapped a hand over his mouth to keep from bursting out.

The speech went on:

"...and some of us are connected in ways that we don't even realize yet."

I bit my tongue, smiling to myself, "Man, you just said a mouthful."

My friend's great white smile widening, he watched me walk over to the speaker who had just finished, as people moved off to visit other family members. It was now or never, no sense in waiting. I approached him, not knowing what his reaction would be. Hesitantly I uttered the words that were going to become the opening phrases of numerous conversations over the next few years.

"You know, I think our family trees crossed, a few generations ago. I'm just finding that out."

Without hesitation, and with a big genuine smile, he extended his hand and said simply,

"Welcome to the family!"

I was elated. I had made contact, and things were continuing to fall into place. I wandered through the tombstones looking at the names. So many of them bore names that were taking shape on my family tree. I stopped at a Barnes stone, scrutinized it for some clue, some signal in the date, in the spirit of the stone. I wasn't alone. Another man, an African-American, was looking at the same stone.

"That name is familiar" said I.

"Well, there are more." Said he. "But they're not here, they're in Deerfield. That's where my great grandmother Sarah Barnes is buried."

I gathered up the courage to say,

"I know that one Sarah Barnes is buried there, but I haven't found the grave yet. She was my great grand aunt. Sarah was my great grandfather's sister. She's buried with her husband William, and her own mother, Betsy Strong. You and

I may have the same great great grandmother... I think we're related to the same person."

He looked at me askance, and moved off.

His reaction proved to follow one of the two kinds of responses to my discoveries that I experienced: either I was received with an extended hand of welcoming, regardless of my skin color, or I met with passive rejection of a potentially upsetting new face in the family, a white one at that.

A similar reaction came from the white members of the family, as our story was revealing itself bit by bit: the younger people thought it wonderful that we had such a rich, textured background, while those of one generation back were deathly afraid the story was coming out, that the black faces in the family would bring back the scandal and humiliation (in their eyes) they thought they had buried long ago.

Chapter 7

Betsy Strong (1838-1897)

"Let us pause in life's pleasures
And count its many tears
While we all sup sorrow with the poor.
There's a song that will linger
Forever in our ears,
Hard Times come again no more.
'Tis the song, the sigh of the weary
Hard Times, Hard Times come again no more
Many days you have lingered around my cabin door
Oh Hard Times come again no more."

--Stephen Foster

All has fallen quiet in the Jeffrey house. Embers glow in the great fireplace; someone throws a dry pine branch onto the coals, it burns brightly, crackling, sending a trail of sparks up the throat of the chimney. Outside, the drums have fallen silent hours ago.

A soft melody comes from the edge of the mill pond, perhaps the fluting of a thrush or a dove, perhaps notes from a wooden flute. Pale light already shows in the east, when a tall form steps toward the fire. A slender woman hesitantly glances at us, taking us in without blinking. Her gaze is steady, though her eyes sparkle with some hidden mischief, as if welling up from deep inside. She has taken up the Talking Stick, looking at it, turning it over and over in her hands, as if puzzled. Her features are strangely familiar: straight nose, high cheekbones, dark braided hair framing her face, skin the color of light copper, broad forehead, slight crease at the bridge of her nose. She begins her story:

37

"Well now. My, my. Where do I start? My grandmother Rebecca had told me about this house, but I never did come here in my lifetime. It is strange to be here now, but I will enjoy talking with you for I do know who you are, and I'm happy to see how this is all turning out. Because it could've been worse. You know me now as Betsy. I have been long forgotten, for a hundred years or more, but I have been waiting here all along, and I'm glad my children's great -grandchildren have been seeking me. So now I'm here and I can tell you my story so that it will not be lost, so the children to come will not forget my name, I will no longer be called Name Cannot Be Known.

I can first remember, when I was three or four years old, we all lived where my father farmed Indian land in Lyme. That would have been around 1840. My father is John Mason Strong and he was born in 1797, so you see, we go back a long way, even farther than that, as you have heard. My mother is Judith Mason, born in 1800. We lived among our own people, and there were so many Masons, Strongs, and Jeffreys between Lyme and East Haddam, it was hard to keep it straight, to keep from marrying your own cousin! My mother Judith came down from the Masons and the Jeffreys. It was her mother, my grandmother Rebecca, who told me about this place in Narragansett, when I was a little girl. All the Masons, the Strongs, the Jeffreys are Indian. We have quite a mix of Niantic, Narragansett, Pequot, Mohegan blood lines. I couldn't even begin to tell you for sure which we really are, probably all of them. I think Grandfather William Mason is part African too but I don't know for sure. We have all that mixed in. Grandmother Rebecca keeps all that in her head. When she left for the spirit world, we just remembered we were Indians. We had to stick together, because although most folks treated us right, it was always hard for people like us. They gave us names like mulatto, Black, Free People of Color. It didn't matter to me, but I was later told it was a way of not calling us Indians, so it was easier to make us disappear.

Father farmed as best he could, and we all had to help him, be out there with him, but I didn't mind. I always liked being outside, I was never much of a housekeeper. It was much better out in the fields. I liked seeing new people come along the road and stop by the fence, they always had stories and news.

By the time I turned fourteen, we had moved around a lot, always one place after another. We moved from Branford where I was born in 1838, to Lyme, from there to New Haven, then we started north to Wallingford and up the river to Windsor.

About then, that's when things got complicated for me. Got myself in trouble, can't say as I could help it. Boys started coming around me pretty early, mostly mixed bloods and colored like we all were, but then along came William. He used to stop by the fields where Father and I and the others were working, and my, he was handsome. He was a tall strange man, with such white skin, so smooth-looking and it seemed like there was some kind of light inside him. He sure was different from any boy I had known before.

He told all kinds of stories, first he said he was a boatman on the river, then he said his father had a farm, sometimes he said he worked over in the city of Hartford. I didn't know what was what or even what was true, but I didn't care.

He had such a way of talking, and I was so young I couldn't help but feel like he was weaving a spell almost. He told me lots of stories about towns he visited up and down the Connecticut. He had such a nice way of laughing. I felt so good that he was paying a lot of attention to me. He had such a way about him and he talked so smooth and low, not rough like some of the boys.

That summer we went together out into a corner of the field a lot. He made me feel good, he made me laugh. I'd say that was the summer I came of age.

He'd talk about him and me getting married and maybe going off to live in the city.

I do say he was a handsome man, and I was sure I would stay with him forever. Guess I should've known better, but I was just a girl back then. He should've known better too, being so much older than me.

Then something bad happened about the time I knew I was going to have William's baby. Of course I thought it would all work out, but what did I know back then?

William stopped coming around, and just plain disappeared. Father heard from some of the boatmen that Will fell into the Connecticut River up near Windsor Locks, but they never found him. It seemed impossible that at my age I could already be a widow woman.

Then somebody else said maybe he was gone off to New York City. I was pretty sure he'd come back for me when he got settled. But he never did. That did break my heart, but it wasn't for the last time. I was never to see him again, not in my lifetime, not even in this world I live in now. That is very strange.

He went and left me with my baby boy. All I knew was at least I had a son. He would be good company and would grow up to take care of me when I got old. I called him Judah William Smith, both after my mother Judith, and his own father that he would never see.

We sure got tired of moving around from place to place on this river. Father was a good farmer, so we always had something to eat, but he sure would have liked his own place.

Too bad, us Masons and Strongs, seemed like moving from place to place was going to be our lot. Grandmother Rebecca Jeffrey's family was better off, they had a nice house in Hartford by then, but we just couldn't get settled. They still called us Free People of Color, but at one point when the census-man came to the door, he put us down as mulattos. Same difference I guess. I didn't care what they called us, I just wished we could stay in one place, find a better life somewhere!

I was doing fine with Judah, Mother, Father and my brother Solomon. I was only seventeen when along came Elijah William Sharpe. He was almost as funny as my own Will Smith, and just as sweet talking, but my, he was dark. I didn't mind so much whatever he was. I could tell he was getting sweet on me. Father didn't mind him being around, because he was such a good worker and told lots of stories. He always carried a fiddle around with him and could get everybody dancing and jumping whenever he wanted. He was easy to like and got me feeling about him like I used to feel about Will. Guess he helped me forget for awhile. Wasn't long before I was in that way again.

Elijah stayed around for some time, long enough to see my little Sarah born. She was a dark one like Elijah himself, darker than anybody else in the family.

Elijah tried his hand at being a barber, but just couldn't settle down. Pretty soon, he drifted down to his father's town on the Mohegan lands. Then I heard he signed up on a ship, maybe a whaling ship like other Mohegans. One day he just sailed away, fiddle and all.

So now I had two little ones on my hands, and we all of us living under one roof in Windsor. We were making ends meet, but just barely. My father was working awfully hard, and lucky for us, my brother Solomon didn't have a lazy bone in his body. He worked just as hard as a grown man, and lots of white folks came around wanting to hire him at harvest time. That helped the family a lot because Father was already sixty-three and couldn't do as much he used to do.

Around about then, I met a fine-looking man, Charles H. Scott. Light skinned like me even though he had some Pequot and black in him somewhere, he certainly seemed different. He had been in the Secession War, in the Navy, and sailed all over I guess. By then I had learned a thing or two. I had lost both my William then Elijah. I was going to marry this man, and do it like the Church wanted us to. So we got married in November 1866 down in Wallingford. Wasn't long before I had two more sons, by Charles. I had little Charles born just after we got married and then came baby Solomon named after my brother, born in 1869.

So there I was with four children now, and a legally married husband. We all changed our name to Scott when that happened. Judah became a Scott around about when he was eighteen, Sarah did too at fifteen. Of course Charles' sons had their father's name.

We had pretty much settled in Wallingford at my father's place, where Charlie worked at farming along with all of us. Brother Solomon was there too, but he was getting anxious to move out on his own. He always was an ambitious one. Those old Indian stories about a beautiful spot up the river further still had stuck with him. He heard the stories from the elders when he was small, about a place so beautiful that it seemed like maybe it wasn't true. Something was pulling Sol to that spot. He had to see it, maybe settle there if it was a place he liked, if the fields and corn were all that the old folks said.

He had to go to Deerfield."

Light of day was gaining on the darkness in the room, the embers glowing and fading out. A kingfisher rattled on the pond, jays called harshly to one another. All of us were weary after this long night of stories. We were drained and exhausted. Betsy spoke to us before leaving.

"It's time to go now. I haven't finished my story yet. But I tell you, when I come to meet you again it'll not be here in Rhode Island in this house of the ancestor Joseph. I will meet you in the home of my son Judah, up in Massachusetts in the beautiful valley near where I lived out my days. I am comfortable there, even with his wife Lizzie's fussing and stern looks, it is the homestead I yearned for. I'll leave the Talking Stick here, I can talk pretty good without it".

She glanced at us with that mischievous look again, as she stepped out and away into time.

* * *

Considerable time had passed, months maybe, but those of us who stayed in the family circle knew that we had to meet soon, so that Betsy could come back and finish what she needed to say.

In early fall, we are gathered in Judah's house along the river, built in 1872. From Joseph Jeffrey's house in Rhode Island, to Judah's house in Massachusetts, one Indian house to another. Two bookends to a story.
There's a warm fire in the massive 1912 Glenwood C Cookstove, coffee keeping warm on the stovetop. A cat sprawled contentedly under the stove, gangly yellow dog snuggles her head near the cat. There's no tobacco, no sweetgrass, just the rich aroma of coffee. The parlor is lit in the

pale light from the oil lamp, as we want it. We are waiting, expecting that Betsy will come, but there's no way of knowing. She said she would come when we were ready. Chairs are drawn up in a circle in the parlor near the stove.

Then at last, that familiar face last seen at the Jeffrey house appears, same thin-lipped smile, same deep light in her dark eyes. She's not alone. A very tall man with a goatee, bowler hat in hand, is standing beside her, as well as a dark-skinned girl with straight long braids, prominent, determined chin. Betsy has brought her children here with her to the homestead, now our home, as she said she would.

She takes a seat near the stove, her children draw up chairs. The Talking Stick was left in the Jeffrey house, no longer needed, so far from the homeland, so far from her people.

She looks slowly around the room, hums a tune in a distracted way, singing to herself:

"...There's a song that will linger
Forever in our ears
Hard Times come again no more...."

Her faint voice trails off, as she looks at each of us in turn. We are her great -great grandchildren gazing at her across the years.

"I'm so glad to be in this house with all my kin around me. This is where I always felt best, this is the family's lasting home after all those generations of wandering and never settling. Judah found us a place we could keep.

But you want to hear the rest of my story, and I want to tell it, so that it will not be forgotten, so that our names can be known and remembered. Now where was I?

Well, back then, Solomon was getting to be twenty-two or so, and like all young men, he wanted to see life and get ahead. He was tired of moving around and never putting down roots. Of course our people always moved from place to place anyway, but times were changing, the War was over, and there was a feeling of promise everywhere. Solomon heard of the valley to the north, sounded like it might be perfect for us. Of course we had a recollection of Deerfield because the old people talked about it from time to time as a place of rich land, great meadows, where the best corn grows, where there could be more space for somebody like Solomon, maybe Judah too, maybe all of us.

So Solomon set out alone upriver to see if he couldn't find a new home, make a new start, and stay put. He was a handsome tall man and it didn't take long before he found a good solid wife, Matilda Beauchamp, down from up north in Canada. Sol was busy getting a place to live and he sent for all of us.

We didn't need to be asked twice, so pretty quick, we all found passage on a river boat, couldn't afford the train, and up to Deerfield and Cheapside we went. There was Father John Mason Strong already almost seventy-five, Mother, me and the four children. Judah was almost twenty-one, Sarah now in her eighteenth year, and little Charles and Solomon. It was hard, because my husband Charles wouldn't come north with us. He was proud and stubborn. He was a New Haven man and after his time in the War he didn't want to pull up stakes and move again. His brother Rudolph had headed west and was making a name for himself out in Spokane. But Charles was tired, getting sickly, and he just wouldn't come. But we went anyway, and he stayed behind. We were meant to go, and he was meant to stay. Poor Charles died only a few years later, in 1876, down there, so there I was a widow woman at only thirty-eight. But I was in Deerfield.

The stories were all true, there were great meadows, rich land. Solomon had found us a place to live on Deerfield Road, where we could look out on the fields along the Deerfield River. That road led to towns in either direction. Up to Greenfield or down across the river by ferry to Deerfield town.

We liked Deerfield just fine with its wide streets and fields coming right up to the great houses there, but most of us liked Greenfield even better. More hustle and bustle there, the young ones certainly preferred that. Judah was getting pretty good with horses and before long he met up with Levi Gunn, who had a fine house on Main Street.

Mr. Levi offered him a job driving his carriage, even got Sarah a job too working in the house. That's when Judah's fortunes started looking up. High time too, he was getting to be close to twenty-six.

Both Judah and Sarah got married in 1881. Judah married Elizabeth Moir, a handsome Scottish woman just come over from Aberdeen. She was good for Judah, he was so headstrong, but she could outdo him for all that. I could tell though, she didn't care too much for me, and poor Sarah was too dark-skinned for that Lizzie, I'll say. She was a strict Calvinist Protestant, and right from the start she ruled that household with an iron hand, but I suppose that wasn't so bad. Judah was so big, over six foot and she was so small, but she didn't let that stop her! By and by, she had a house full of boys, so she needed to be strong.

Times were tough, times were hard, but I guess what they say about the Scots is true. Lizzie was as thrifty as they come, and they all turned out right. My Sarah married too, a few months after Judah and Elisabeth. Married a nice white man named William Barnes. He had gotten wounded in the War, and so Sarah collected a good widow's pension for years after her poor William had died. They had five boys, and no girls. Judah and Lizzie had six boys too, and one daughter, little Ida.

So those years had some joys mixed in with some sorrows. I was a widow, and my mother Judith a widow too. But I still had my boys Solomon and Charles, and both Judah and Sarah were starting to get ahead. I must count my joys really, and leave the sorrows be, because what with all our moving about before, we had found a home for us all finally in this fine valley here. Judah got himself this nice house near the river and pasture lands, not far from me. Once a month or so he'd come and get me and bring me here for a spell. Sometimes he took Sarah too.

When you are in your son's house, you feel right at home. Judah and I had been through a lot together, me being such a young girl when he was born. My Sarah with her beautiful skin from Elijah was just as smart as a whip besides being so beautiful. What with that faraway look in her eyes, you could tell she could see things the rest of us couldn't.

I'd say I moved around a lot especially after Mother died in 1883. Sometimes I stayed with Sarah, sometimes on my own here and there. I was feeling strangely tired much of the time, even though I had years to go to catch up with Mother and Father who had lived out such long lives before they passed away.

By 1888, the year of the great blizzard, my son Solomon Scott had married a nice girl, Isabella, and then my son Charles got married too. He met Cornelia Smith up in Charlemont and married. They gave me four grandsons and I was glad they named one of them Charles, both after his father and his grandfather, my Charles H. Scott. I know now later on they had another son Solomon, that's a nice name. I guess he was named for my brother Solomon Strong, and Solomon Scott too.

I have to say I was weary by 1896, I didn't know there was something in me going to take my life within the year. I was ready to go, you know when it's your time, but I knew all along from the old people that I wouldn't really be gone. I could come back to visit maybe, help out, tell stories, remind kin of where we come from, kind of like now.

They put me in the ground in Deerfield in 1897, I was glad to get some rest. I had reached this spot which was my fate after all.

Looking back, I can see the line of stepping stones from there to here, those old Nehantic people we come from. Joseph, then George Jeffrey, Cooley Mason and Stepney Strong, my mother's mother Rebecca Jeffrey Mason, they all lead down to me and down to you here.

Only one more thing I have to tell though, I get so angry about this Name Cannot Be Known business. I'm glad you're getting the story straight now. I stuck it out. I did start up four families, you know. Each of my children gave me lots of descendants, including you all right here. You're here because of me.

So you'll remember me, won't you? I'll be grateful if you remember me, I don't want to be Name Cannot Be Known any longer. I'm Betsy Strong, and don't you forget me."

Bits of her song linger in her fading smile, quiet settles into the room, the oil lamp still burns its yellow light.

"...There are frail forms waiting at the door,
Though their voices are silent,

Their hopeful looks will say,
Oh, Hard Times come again no more...."

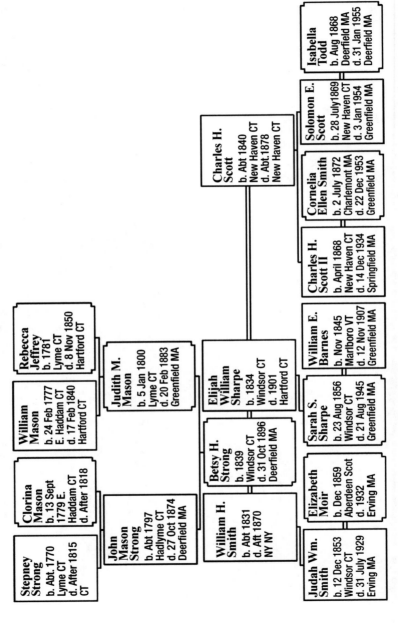

Betsy H. Strong

Stepney Strong
b. Abt. 1770
Lyme CT
d. After 1815 CT

Clorina Mason
b. 13 Sept 1779 E.
Haddam CT
d. After 1818

William Mason
b. 24 Feb 1777
E. Haddam CT
d. 17 Feb 1840
Hartford CT

Rebecca Jeffrey
b. 1781
Lyme CT
d. 8 Nov 1850
Hartford CT

John Mason Strong
b. Abt 1797
Hadlyme CT
d. 27 Oct 1874
Deerfield MA

Judith M. Mason
b. 5 Jan 1800
Lyme CT
d. 20 Feb 1883
Greenfield MA

Charles H. Scott
b. Abt 1840
New Haven CT
d. Abt. 1878
New Haven CT

William H. Smith
b. Abt 1831
d. Aft 1870
NY NY

Betsy H. Strong
b. 1839
Windsor CT
d. 31 Oct 1896
Deerfield MA

Elijah William Sharpe
b. 1834
Windsor CT
d. 1901
Hartford CT

Charles H. Scott II
b. April 1868
New Haven CT
d. 14 Dec 1934
Springfield MA

Cornelia Ellen Smith
b. 2 July 1872
Charlemont MA
d. 22 Dec 1953
Greenfield MA

Solomon E. Scott
b. 28 July1869
New Haven CT
d. 3 Jan 1954
Greenfield MA

Isabella Todd
b. Aug 1868
Deerfield MA
d. 31 Jan 1955
Deerfield MA

Judah Wm. Smith
b. 12 Dec 1853
Windsor CT
d. 31 July 1929
Erving MA

Elizabeth Moir
b. Dec 1859
Aberdeen Scot
d. 1932
Erving MA

Sarah S. Sharpe
b. 23 Aug 1856
Windsor CT
d. 21 Aug 1945
Greenfield MA

William E. Barnes
b. Nov 1845
Marlboro VT
d. 12 Nov 1907
Greenfield MA

Chapter 8

Deerfield 2008

Pocumtuck, the area now known as Deerfield, was named for the tribe that inhabited this part of the valley when the first Europeans came. Somewhere around 1670 Pocumtuck became Deerfield. It does have an ancient and historic resonance to it. The calm, tree-shaded Main Street is lined with early colonial homes, replicas or originals that evoke the earliest days of the settlement here, when Deerfield was the last outpost on the New England frontier. At the northern end of Main Street lie a hundred acres of fields bordering the Deerfield River, and beyond, in the eyes of the Protestant population of the 1600s, lay the wilderness reaching up to Quebec, peopled only by hostile tribes and perfidious French Catholics.

The history and the name of this settlement are irrevocably entwined with the Raid of 1704, when on February 29th, the snows had blown up into drifts that permitted the raiding band of Abenaki, Mohawk, Huron and Pocumtucks to scale the palisade and open the gates to the rest of their band and the French officers.

Captives that night were marched off to Quebec to be ransomed if they survived the trek. Many didn't. Some were ransomed, others chose to stay among their captors, finding more freedom and independence in the tribal life style than they ever would have in the severe Protestant society of Deerfield.

Since the beginning of colonial settlement here, Deerfield was synonymous with white America's early struggle with the elements, of which tribal people were a part. The English are often portrayed as brave early settlers fighting to survive in this valley, staking a claim in empty God-given territory, resisting harsh winters and hostile Indians.

But there is another perspective. The dimension of Deerfield that was Pocumtuck has been minimized by some historians, yet there is a 12,000 year history that had been overlooked until recently. Deerfield, before being given that name, was a homeland for tribal people. That tree-lined main street with its Liberty Pole and Inn, was a native path leading to fields cleared by native people and north to Abenaki lands. This was a pivotal, ancient pathway for the First People, who in annual seasonal movement stopped in this spot to meet, to plant and harvest corn, to plan war or make peace. Peskeompskut was only six miles away, at the place where the rock had split the river, creating the great falls where shad and salmon were harvested, and where peoples of many nations met in truce. Pocumtuck was a destination, a homeland, a place of exceptional beauty and spirituality.

Deerfield. I should have known that the trail would lead me here. How else to explain that strange pull this place has had on me since early childhood? Just one valley over from Judah's homestead where we now live, its stately street reminds us all that you can go there and find history, get in touch with something in our past. Yet for me it always seemed there was more to it than that.

Something in the atmosphere, some ancient feeling, some force, some magnetism always pulled me there. Of course, I'm not the only one drawn to Deerfield. We've all read book after book of one of the most studied and researched spots in New England. Maybe this *is* America's hometown. Yet, there is also an uncomfortable atmosphere of elitism that pervades these patrician Yankee streets. Not many of us can be counted among the founding "Deerfield Families" of Anglo-Saxon origin. I've always felt the outsider, the interloper here, with simply a fascination for the time warp of old places. What else but that fascination could explain the weekly drive over to the Deerfield Bookstore or a long walk through the meadows and cornfields? More often than not a winter walk was most evocative, in a simplified ancient landscape when the sun hangs low on the valley rim, the white fields aglow in the pale yellow or salmon pink January sky.

But now, I'm learning that the story and the trail of my own family lead here. Could it be, that just three generations ago, I was placed here, and until now didn't even know it? I'm finding that my *own* people were here too, although they were invisible for the most part. I was beginning to understand why I was drawn here, all those years since childhood. I was learning that my own people had lived and farmed here. And if they had been drawn to Deerfield from tribal lands to the south along the Connecticut River, couldn't it be that their people, my kinsmen, had visited and dwelt in this mystical spot, their homeland, over the millennia?

I began walking taller in those Yankee streets and fields, cleared after all, by Indians.

I was descended from those ancient ancestors who knew Deerfield when it was the Pocumtuck Homeland.

Somehow, Judah and his extended family were drawn back here, living invisible lives on the margins of Deerfield society. They had been drawn back, after generations of displacement in the 1800s , moving throughout the southern Connecticut River Valley from Lyme on Nehantic lands, to New Haven, to Wallingford and Hartford, to Windsor and finally to this spot. What brought them here? Wasn't it family connections, multigenerational memory, oral history of the ancient trails that lead here to this key place in the seasonal movements of tribal people?

So indeed, the trail leads to Deerfield. The records of the 1870s place my kinsfolk, then called mulatto and Free People of Color, here in this town. Judah, his three siblings, Sarah, Charles and Solomon, his mother Betsy Strong, his aunt and uncle Solomon and Matilda Strong, their ten children, plus his grandparents John Mason Strong and Judith Mason, all my multiracial extended family, all resided in Deerfield. How could I not feel grounded here? Their presence explained the pull of this place; their toil, sorrows, ashes and dust are here in this place called Deerfield. Somewhere. Where did they live? What did they do here? Where are they buried?

The search led to the library in Old Deerfield, the Town Offices in South Deerfield, and the cemetery.

David Bosse, the librarian at the Historic Deerfield Library looked up.

"I'm looking for some of my family who may have lived here in the 1870s" I told him.

Although I was probably one of hundreds per year who come through looking for ancestors to connect them with Deerfield's first families (next best thing to tracing back to the Mayflower!), the man was patient, and directed me to George Sheldon's History of Deerfield, old street lists, and the tax records on microfiche.

It's a strange sensation indeed to be sitting in a quiet library on a rainy summer afternoon, and to peel back the pages, the years of your own history and your own destiny. Rain fell softly on the lawn outside the Deerfield Memorial Library, and on the timeless clapboard colonial houses down the street.

With one hand cranking, I was scanning the tax rolls from one hundred and forty years ago, deciphering the ancient handwriting, peering at the shadowy microfiche flickering by like an old time silent movie, when slowly the faint image of the name Judah Smith materialized before my eyes. In the impeccable penmanship of 19th century plume and ink, it was recorded in 1878 that Judah Smith of Deerfield paid a tax of one dollar on a pig. I figured he was twenty-five at the time.

By 1879 he had been taxed on two pigs. We were moving up! There was his name, placing him, and his uncle Solomon Strong on the Deerfield tax rolls. We had picked up the trail, after the census of 1870 that had placed him in Windsor, Ct. He had now in the past eight years moved up the river to Deerfield where he was working at getting a new start. Other records showed that he lived next door to one G.B. Sheldon in the section of Deerfield called Cheapside, overlooking the north meadows along the Deerfield River.

From the library, we left the village and headed to the town hall in South Deerfield.

I chose to follow the old river road along the Connecticut, imagining that was the road traveled on by Judah, Betsy, Solomon and the whole extended family sometime after 1870 as they came up the road to Deerfield. Or perhaps they came up here by boat. The river still flows slowly and broadly along these fertile meadows just like they would have seen it a hundred and forty years ago.

The beginning of this road crosses up over the hill past Laurel Hill Cemetery and Eaglebrook School down over the crest of Pocumtuck Mountain to what seems a secret valley and ancient landscape along the river. The fields were alive with the imagined memory of my ancestors traveling through here by wagon or riverboat up the river from Windsor to Cheapside.

This road, this day, eventually led me in a round-about way to the Town Offices.

The cheery, pleasant Town Clerk handed me the five pound bound book of records of births, marriages, and deaths recorded in the town between 1870 and 1897. By now I knew who I was looking for: anyone by the name of Strong, Scott, or Barnes.

The first name to appear was John Mason Strong, who died in October of 1874. He was Betsy's father, Judah's grandfather, and my three times great-grandfather. He was seventy-seven at the time of his death, which would give him a birth year of 1797. He was born in Lyme, Connecticut. I had already learned that at various times in his life he was listed on the census as a Free Person of Color, sometimes mulatto, sometimes black. But this record of his death connected him to all those names associated with the Nehantic tribe and Lyme: Joseph Jeffrey, George and Rebecca Jeffrey, Cooley Mason and Stepney Strong, and on down to me. All this family history, all these secrets, were lying in the dark books of record all these years, waiting to be rediscovered, to come alive.

Further entries showed the tragic disappearances of three of his grandchildren. John Mason Strong's son Solomon Strong and his wife Matilda lost a daughter Anna Elizabeth in a fire in 1875, sons Elijah and John Mason Strong II were lost to typhoid in 1882.

Finally, on the last page I found *her*: Betsy H. Strong, Judah's mother. She was lost to cancer. She died at the age of fifty-eight in 1897. I knew she held the key to much of the mystery in the family, the story of where we came from, how I came to be in this place.

But so much still seemed to be unknowable.

Now I needed to find her final resting place. She was not in the Green River Cemetery with her mother Judith and her father John. Maybe she was with her daughter Sarah Sharp Barnes? We needed to look in Deerfield.

A small family group, Allen, Barbara and I, composed our search team. We gathered early one afternoon in November, and fanned out in the Old Deerfield Cemetery. Records showed that Sarah and her husband were buried somewhere in Deerfield. The old slate tombstones of the first white settlers were holding up as well as could be expected under the centuries.

Deerfield boys and girls of privilege, from the Academy, played their various fall sports below in the fields, confident, aristocratic, and loud in the distance.

We continued searching for some sign of a neglected, long-lost family of poor colored folks somewhere among these stones. We paused briefly before the burial mound of the victims of the Deerfield Raid of 1704, tragic in its loss of life both for the white settlers and the tribal people seeking to win back their native homeland of Pocumtuck.

Barbara and I mused respectfully that we had actually descended from some of the attackers; we had mutual ancestors both French, Huron, and Abenaki who had participated in the 1704 raid.

We were getting nowhere however; none of the tombstones had dates indicating burials occurred here anytime after the 1850s.

The daylight wasn't going to last long this dark November afternoon. The days were growing quickly shorter. That day the sun was already a brilliant orange ball near the western horizon. Then it occurred to me that I had passed another cemetery on my round-about way to the Town Offices a month ago. Of course! The Laurel Hill Cemetery! It was up on the hill, overlooking the town, just off the road that leads over the notch to the banks of the Connecticut.

Once again, we fanned out in search of a familiar name, the one we were looking for. It's a quiet lovely place, this cemetery on a hill sloping downwards to the trees. No noise, a few crows calling on the way to their evening roosting place. Stones with Yankee, Polish, French, English, German surnames, polished bright, decorated with fall flowers and flags, upright in neat rows, of course.

It was Barbara who spotted it first.

Down the slight hill, on the edge of the dark ravine, all alone in the poorest corner, on the least desirable plot, stood the stone.

"Barnes" was the name the tombstone carried.

We approached it slowly, hearts in our throats, not daring to hope. Stepping around to view the names of those in this grave, there she was: *Betsy Strong*! Her name was placed in the center of the stone, along with the names of her daughter Sarah, Sarah's husband William Barnes, as well as their sons.

We were overwhelmed by this discovery, as has happened at every turning in this story. What do you do when your people long forgotten show themselves to you? They're here, almost lost to all memory, except no longer lost, not now. To think I have passed by this spot on the well-traveled road below, all my 60 years, never knowing my own people were resting just up the hill, alone in this humble and precarious grave.

Betsy had been brought here, in 1897, by Judah, his sister Sarah, brothers Charles and Solomon, the whole extended family.

Had they come back over the years? Someone in the families had to have known. One by one, Sarah's sons had been laid to rest here with their father, mother, and grandmother, right up to 1985. They had served in WWI in the Pioneer Division, segregated troops in Woodrow Wilson's war.

The stone was tilted, the flags ragged, and no flag at all flew over William who had fought in the Civil War with his Vermont Regiment, for the Union, and for the future of People of Color. We would get him his flag, too. But at least now we knew where they all were, they would be visited again, and their stories never forgotten, this time.

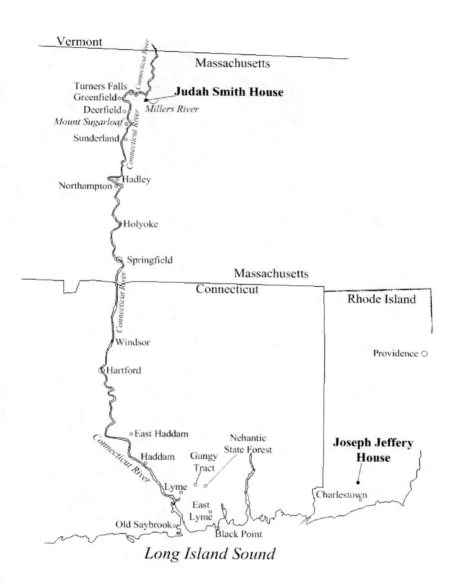

The Southern Connecticut River Valley

From Charlestown, Rhode Island to Millers Falls, Massachusetts
1700–2014

Judah W. Smith Family
Douglas, William, Clinton, Perry,
Elizabeth (Moir), Alan, Judah W. Smith
circa 1900

Judah W. Smith Family in 1888

Ida (1886–1890), Judah, William,
Elizabeth (Moir), Clinton, and Charlie (1885-1894) Smith

Judah W. Smith, Millers Falls Company
Erving, MA circa 1890–1920

Judah Smith and Elizabeth Moir Smith
circa 1904

Judah and Elizabeth
circa 1928

Solomon Elijah Strong Family

Above: **Eleanor J. Strong**
1874–1964

Left: **Matilda Strong**
1888–1951

Grace Strong
1886–1968

Nine children were born into the Solomon Elijah Strong family in Deerfield, MA. Solomon was Betsy Strong's brother, so his children were her nieces and nephews.

Left: **George Lorman Strong**
1878–1959

Douglas W. Smith
1892–1973
Son of Judah and
Elizabeth Smith

Sarah (Sharpe) Barnes
1856–1945
Judah Smith's half sister

Alan C. Smith
1896–1973
Youngest son of Judah and
Elizabeth Smith

**Elizabeth "Pete" (Smith)
Gessing** 1917–1986
Daughter of Alan C. Smith,
granddaughter of Judah Smith

The Joseph Jeffrey House

The Joseph Jeffrey House is an historic house on Old Mill Road in Charlestown, Rhode Island, and is considered significant to the history of Rhode Island architecture. The main part of the house is a 1-1/2 story, wood-frame structure with a gambrel roof, central chimney, and a small gable roof ell to the northeast.

The oldest portion of the main block appears to be the easterly side, which rests on an old stone foundation and exhibits construction methods typical of 18th-century colonial architecture.

The house was built circa 1720 by Joseph Jeffrey, a Narragansett and a member of Ninigret's Tribal Advisory Council.

The house was added to the National Register of Historic Places in 1978, an early example of the acceptance of the colonists' cultural standards by an important member of the indigenous population.

Another view of the house is on the cover. Photos by Monique Brule.

Donald Scott and David Brule

Page No. 53

SCHEDULE 1.—Free Inhabitants in *Windsor* in the County of *Hartford* State of *Connecticut* enumerated by me, on the *21* day of *June* 1860. *Gilbert Clark* Ass't Marshal

Post Office *Poquonock.*   Race M = Mulatto

		The name of every person whose usual place of abode on the first day of June, 1860, was in this family.				Profession, Occupation, or Trade of each person, male and female, over 15 years of age.	Value of Real Estate.	Value of Personal Estate.	Place of Birth, Naming the State, Territory, or Country.				Whether deaf and dumb, blind, insane, idiotic, pauper, or convict.	
1	2	3	4	5	6	7	8	9	10	11	12	13	14	
33				m	M							14		33
36	271	422	*John M Strong*	63			*Farmer*							36
37			*Judith M.*	60	F									37
38			*Betsy H.*	21										38
39			*Coleman E.*	12	m							14		39
40			*Judah Smith*	7	m							14		40
1			*Sarah L Strong*	4	F				*Conn*			1		1
			No. white males, *15* No. colored males, *4* No. foreign born, ___ No. blind, ___				7,600	14	No. idiotic, ___				No. convict, ___	
			No. white females, *14* No. colored females, *2* No. deaf and dumb, ___ No. insane, ___						No. pauper, ___					

Census of 1860

David Brule and Donald Scott
At the Narragansett Church, August 2010

Chapter 9

Judah Smith (1853-1929)
Elizabeth Moir Smith (1859-1932)
Sarah Sharpe Barnes (1856-1945)

We were now used to these long evenings of story-telling, when the ancestors came to tell us about their lives. We had, at Betsy's insistence, moved our meetings from the distant Jeffrey house in Narragansett country in Rhode Island, to Judah's house in Massachusetts where we, her family, still lived.

The house had fallen silent. The clock ticked on the shelf in the kitchen, over the table. The lamplight glowed yellow and bright. Outside, the mourning doves fluted in the gathering dusk, the wood thrush was waiting for the early evening to sing his trills and vibrato.

A familiar, gaunt man cleared his throat.

There he was finally.

Given the nature of time, I felt I've been following his trail since before I was born, before he was born, down through the lines of Joseph Jeffrey, Cooley Mason, William and Rebecca Mason, to Judith and Betsy. From the Narragansett and Niantics in Charlestown to Lyme, up and down the river until finally reaching Deerfield and Millers Falls. I've been on his trail for 300 years. And now there he was before us, in his own parlor, in my parlor. We came face to face with Judah.

Tall and lanky, long arms and massive hands, straight and dignified, haughty even, high cheek bones, straight nose, broad forehead, something strange and different about the eyes. He set his bowler hat on his knees, flattened his sparse hair with one hand. His voice came forth slow and rich, from somewhere deep in his chest, baritone maybe, a voice rich with

71

flavor from a lifetime spent in between the communities of colored folks and of white folks.

"Well, I'm here. Good thing too, for me, and for you. I'll tell you what you want to know, as best I can."

His eyes narrowed at the corners, eyelids closing down to mere slits shining in the lamplight as he remembered.

"I came into this world in 1853, as far as I know. Mother was young when I was born. That kind of kept us close all these years. She was just a girl of fourteen. She had great love for my father, William, but I never got to know him. Disappeared even before I was one year old. Drowned in the river they told me when I was old enough to ask. She gave me his name for a middle name. I gave his name to my first-born son. Guess he was probably white unlike the rest of us, but she never said much else other than to praise him and cry sometimes. She was a good woman, Betsy Strong. And a good mother.

Before long, when I was about three years old, a little sister came along, Sarah here. Mother and a dark man, Elijah, Sarah's father, were married for a spell. He helped her forget. But he didn't stick around long. And then there we were, Mother, Sarah, and me. 'Course Grandmother and Grandfather were there too, Judith and John Mason Strong.

Not much changed when little Sarah was born, we all just stayed together under one roof. That's how it was with our people. Family's family, kin is kin. It's just what people did. Least that's what *we* did anyway.

Just after the Secession War, Mother met a fine man. That was Charles H. Scott. He and Mother got married in the church, the way more and more of our people were doing when they decided to stay together.

They had two children by and by, two brothers for me and Sarah. Their names were Charles, for my stepfather, and Solomon, for my uncle. My stepfather changed our family name to Scott, at least for a while.

He had been in the War, and told us all kinds of stories about what he did during those times. He was considered colored, like all of us who weren't exactly white. Said his grandfather was a Pequot chief who married a Scotswoman. Just about everybody in those days had some black mixed in there too. Don't know much about it, never asked.

So Charles, my stepfather, kept us entertained with war stories. He was quite a storyteller I'd say. He was in the Union Navy, where colored folks mixed in with whites easier than in other outfits, besides they liked to take Indians from the coast into the navy. Seems like that's what Indians liked best too. He went all over the place on his ship, the USS Sabine. Even over to Africa and back, looking for the ships the Rebs had. Even got wounded, and never really got over it, bothered him for the rest of his life.

So, we were one big family of Scotts for a few years, but that wasn't going to last. My uncle Solomon Strong began getting itchy to move north up the Connecticut Valley. He heard all his life about the rich land and open fields up there, up north of Springfield, up to Deerfield, so he was going up there to see if he liked it. For us, it was better than going out West, I guess.

Charles' brother Rudolph went out there and was doing fine, by all accounts. But for some reason, Uncle Sol just wanted to see what was north of Windsor. He was only a few years older than me, and got me itching to go up there too. Even Mother got the urge to move again, though she always said she was tired of getting up and going somewhere else all the time.

That's when some trouble started.

My stepfather Charles didn't want to leave his land and pull up roots again. He was getting sickly, and I have to say that Mother didn't know what to do. She figured she had to stick with him. She's a good woman, don't you think anything bad about her, but she's a high-spirited one for sure. That Indian blood in her just wouldn't let her stay put. It was getting to her, working on her. She needed to move again and go up river with Sol, go up to Deerfield, and that was that. Charles didn't like that, but she said she'd for sure go alone if he didn't want to come, and by God, that's what she did.

Long about 1871 or '72, Solomon got himself married to a nice Frenchwoman from Montreal. They got hitched in Greenfield, and Sol was set on getting a piece of land somewhere up there. Like I was telling you, I was itching to go too, nothing holding me back really.

So b'fore long, I was on a boat going upriver along with everybody else. There we all were, Mother, the two boys, me and Sarah, Grandfather John Mason Strong and Grandmother Judith. Didn't have much belongings, just a couple of trunks.

Well I tell you, that was about the grandest trip I ever had. Getting up north of Springfield, that valley just stretched out flat from the river bank as far as you could see in any direction, couple of hills off in the distance. Grandfather could tell that dirt was rich and deep, he was itching to jump off just to feel it. He didn't have to ask if the land was good, he *knew* it. Those hills off in the distance were nothing like we had down in Windsor, and those fine ridges outside of Northampton were a sight to see.

Once we got through the canals in that town and back on the river, I tell you, it got better and better. We all just sat on the deck and watched it all go by, moving north. Sometimes the boatmen poled us along, shoving their poles down into the mud and walking the length of the deck, other times there was a team of horses that'd pull us along by the towpath.

It was getting dark when we saw that big bluff up around Sunderland called the Sugarloaf. It sure gave Mother a leap in her heart. Said she never saw anything so beautiful. She was humming and smiling, her dark eyes dancing, made her forget we all had to leave Charles behind, and we knew he wasn't too happy about it. Can't explain it to this day, we just all had to go.

We only had a few more miles to go to get to Cheapside, but the captain decided to stop for the night, and make his landing in the morning.

That night Mother and Grandmother took Sarah and the two boys over to a boarding house in Sunderland. Grandfather and I chose to sleep on the cramped deck, under the stars. We wanted to stay close to our trunks and belongings. Besides, I hadn't yet had enough of the river, I liked the smooth rocking of the boat, the wide spread of water, nice and calm, just below that big mountain where we were tied up.

Grandfather and I were enjoying a quiet smoke in the early dusk, sun going down in the West behind that Sugarloaf, moon starting to rise at the same time behind us, coming over the ridge to the East.

Big heron flew slowly downriver, catfish feeding broke the surface from time to time, shiners leaping up and out of the water, all sparkling.

Lying there, stretched out smoking, my grandfather murmuring some kind of a story in between draws on his pipe, we didn't even notice the canoe coming downstream until it brushed the side of the barge.

"Say gents", a dark voice said, "Spare a smoke."

We both raised up on our elbows, leaned a bit to see who was there. A dark man, matching the dark voice, sharp eyes like a crow, peered at us from under a broad-brimmed slouch hat.

Grandfather leaned over and handed him the packet of tobacco.

The dark eyes gleamed and danced.

"Well now! You be John Mason Strong! Way up here! What you up to in this part of the river?"

"Don't reckon as I know you, stranger", said my grandfather.

"I call myself Moosamuttuck, and I'd know John Mason Strong anywhere."

Grandfather looked him over.

"I'll be damned, you Issac Waukeet?"

"That's me. Indian name or English name. Don't matter to me."

"You got my name right. This here is my grandson Judah"

"You lucky, big grandson like that." He turned to me.

"I knew your granddaddy when he was a young buck downriver in Lyme. Long time ago. We had some pretty good times down there."

Grandfather looked a little uncomfortable. This man Moosamattock or Waukeet asked where we were going.

"We're on the way upriver, up yonder. Maybe going to settle up in Deerfield." That's what I told him.

"Ah, you'll like it fine here," said the Indian in the canoe. "This was all ours long time ago. See that big mountain up there? That's the big beaver's head, We-quomps, but the whites call it Sugarloaf now. Back long time ago that beaver

76

was making a nuisance, so the sachems called on ol'Hobbomock to get rid of him. Took his war club and hit him back the head. That be his head right there. You can see the rest of him up longside the river, his tail even reaches almost to Deerfield. Leastwise, that's what we say around here."

He laughed and coughed a bit.

"We had a pretty good fight with the English just over there near the foot of We-quomps too. Couple of times, we whipped them pretty good over there. Very good fight. 'Specially when we win."

He laughed and coughed again.

"But that was long time ago, John Strong. Times are different now. Got to stay out of their way. Stay invisible. They don't like to be reminded of us.

He dipped a paddle and moved off.

"Got to get some catfish tonight or I'll be in plenty trouble with the woman. Good-bye boys, thanks for the smoke."

We settled back onto the deck. Neither of us spoke. Heron winged upstream, moving slow over the water. Beaver arrowed out across the river, silver ripples flowed out from his head in the moonlight.

Judah looked at us as if coming back from some distant place in his mind.

Hm! Don't know where that came from. Haven't thought about it for more'n a hundred years!"

He thought that was pretty funny, and I could see why, given the present circumstance there in the parlor. Then he picked up the thread of his story.

"Well, next morning we pulled up to the docks in the place they called Cheapside, below a stretch of rapids. Called it that name because goods were cheaper right near the docks, and were more expensive in the shops in town. That was the end of the line for us, Solomon was there to take us to his house on the Deerfield Road. Can't say we knew that then, but this was going to be home, at least for some of us.

Over the next few years there, I went about doing the best I could. Solomon and I worked at farming and tending fields. We all had settled on the Deerfield Road, next to G. B. Sheldon, and we had a grand view of those meadows and river, just like Mother always wanted. Sol and Matilda started having children and it sure was getting crowded. Grandfather died in 1874, just plain worn out. That old Indian man had worked hard all his natural life and he needed a rest. One day, he just closed his eyes looking out at the meadows, said a couple of words in a tongue lost long ago, I didn't understand. Yep, he just closed his eyes and that was it.

About the same time, we got word that my stepfather Charles was in a bad way. Wounds from the War, and discouragement from being alone down there in Connecticut wore him down. Mother and the boys went back down the river to see what comfort they could bring, but it t'weren't no good. He was gone by the time they got there, that would've been in 1876.

I stayed put, working with Sol, and we were starting to get ahead. I had a way with horses, but I guess I was none too easy on them either. They worked hard for me, I gave them what they needed, but I could've been easier on them I suppose. Along about 1878 or '79, man named Levi Gunn came around. That's when things started falling into place.

Mr. Gunn was about 50 at the time and he was getting to be plenty well off. He was a clever man with lots of ideas. He had started a company over in Millers Falls after the War and was beginning to make money on it. He had a nice house on Main Street up in Greenfield. Pretty soon he offered me a job taking care of his horses and driving him around town in his carriage, or on trips over the hill to the factory in Millers. When he saw Sarah, and figured out how smart she was, besides being pretty good-looking, he gave her a job in his house too. So there we went, out of the fields and up to a fine house in the center of town. Lots going on up there, and we were glad to get out of Sol's house, get some elbow room.

Mr. Levi Gunn was good to us, in a kind of charitable way. In those days it was often that well-off white folks took in people like us, Indians or colored, to help us get ahead, give us jobs and a little education sometimes. I did all the work, and Sarah got a little bit of writing and reading out of it. I was getting older by then, almost twenty-six, and plenty big. Don't know why, but Levi took a liking to me, and made sure I turned out alright, kept an eye on me for the rest of my life. But other than working for him, we never got out much into town society, especially with the Gunns, for sure. 'Course the few times we did get out on the town, we knew enough to stick with our own kind. The rich folks had their habits and ways, we had ours.

Best times I ever had in those days were with Ol' John Putnam. He lived pretty far down Wells Street, but he had a barber shop on Main Street, up where the department store is now, and he played the fiddle for dances. Mr. Gunn used to go over to John's barber shop for a shave and a haircut. I'd get trimmed up too but never had much of a head of hair, always had more than Uncle Sol but that's not saying a lot.

Have to say there's something about a fiddle though, and soon as I heard my first one I knew I wanted to do what Ol'John did. So when I could, I went down to his house and he showed me how to scratch out a few tunes.

You better watch out, I've been eyeing that fiddle there hanging on the hook in the corner behind you-all, I imagine I'll play a tune or two before I go, it's been a long time.

Anyway, back to what I was saying. John was real black and he was as nice as you could ask. He oftentimes took me along to the dances he played at. I did have some fun, I tell you!

During the Secession War, even before that, John helped a lot of his kind escape further north. Word was that his house on Wells Street was part of the Underground Railroad, and he did once show me a tunnel in the cellar, going somewhere.

So 'bout then, things were looking up. I met Old Put' who showed me how to fiddle, Levi Gunn got me and Sarah a nice clean job, and before long I met up with Lizzie. She come over from Scotland around 1878 and wound up with her kinfolk at Major Keith's house at 2 West Main. Since I was working at 24 Main, sooner or later we were going to meet up.

Of course, looking back, I was spending time with John Putnam and his family, and Sis was awful dark-skinned, and at first, Lizzie didn't know what to make of me! She's mighty small too and I'm over six foot. But she saw something in me, maybe she was desperate, but before long we got ourselves married, March 18, 1881, by Reverend Newell at the Congregational Church.

Mr. Gunn threw us a little party and the whole family came up from Deerfield for it. There was Solomon, Matilda and their kids, Grandmother Judith, Sarah, my brothers the Scott boys Solomon and Charles, the whole bunch. Lizzie only had her cousins the Moirs to stand up for her, and they didn't look none too happy. Them Calvinists don't like to dance much and don't drink either.

I should've known how that was going to be from then on. But I'm not complaining, don't dare! That little bit of a Scotswoman would make me sorry if I did!

John Putnam played at our party a little and we all danced anyway in spite of those Calvinist stick-in-the-muds, so didn't Mr. Gunn and his family. That was when Mr. Gunn took me aside, on my wedding day that was, and said he could set me up driving wagon for his new factory, the Millers Falls Company. He also wanted to show me a house and pasture land. He said that he'd stand up for me with the mortgage. You know I'm talking about this house we're sitting in now.

I'll tell you, Mother was bursting with pride. She kept saying imagine now her own son, married and going to own land after all those years of wandering around like the old Indian folks, now we're going to put down roots in one place. She was probably even more excited than me.

Me and Lizzie were going to settle down in this clapboard house along the river, seven acres of meadow and pasture, nice barn for the stock and a job just up the road. Had to go into debt for $450 to get it, but Levi guaranteed it, and Lizzie's upbringing kept us on track. She couldn't tolerate a debt, couldn't tolerate owing anybody money, so we paid off that mortgage lickety-split, and in four years it was all ours.

Other thing that Mr. Gunn did for me too, a year before my wedding, is that when the census man came to the door, Levi told him I was *white*. I didn't know about it, learned about it later. Didn't seem like much at the time, but looking back, that changed a lot of things for you people that come along later. Couldn't change Sarah though, she was just too dark to be anything else 'cept what she was.

Sarah and her beau were there for the wedding along with everybody else. My, she was pretty that day, nice dress and those sparkling eyes, a big smile. Couple of months later, she got married too, her and William Barnes. Mother was glad we both married white people. She was sure that'd help us get ahead, and for sure it'd help the children that'd come along. Sarah's husband Will had been in the War on the Union side, and he got a wounded man's pension. That'd be something good in their old age.

So by 1882 we'd bought the house and land. Mr. Gunn stood guarantee for me like I said, Lizzie pinched them pennies 'til they turned into dollars, and then pinched the dollars 'til the eagle screamed. We paid off the mortgage fast as can be.

We started having children plenty quick. Took some doing in that marriage bed, her being so small and all, and me with my long legs, but pretty soon along came our firstborn. We called him William, after my own father I never knew, and stuck in Mason for a middle name so we'd never forget Grandfather and Grandmother. By then it'd been years since I was back to calling myself Judah Smith again, and not Judah Scott. After my stepfather Charles' death, we all went back to our old names. Betsy went back to being Betsy Strong like her parents, Sarah went back to Sharpe after Elijah. The younger boys, Solomon and Charles, kept their father's name of Scott. I named my second son Charlie to honor my stepfather Charles Scott who helped raise me. He had been good to me and Mother, to all of us. Too bad he didn't move up to Deerfield with us, maybe things would've turned out different for him, and for us.

Me and Lizzie got our family going right away. Will was born in September 1881 just before we moved into the house. Then along came Charlie, then Perry a few years after that.

Then Clinton, Douglass, Ida, and our last one Alan, in 1896. He was the youngest, the apple of his mother's eye. He's the one somehow everyone started calling Abe. We all filled up this house, I'll tell you. Lizzie ran the whole bunch of us with an iron hand. Not a one stepped out of line or they got a good licking. From Lizzie, or from me, when they got older.

Over in Deerfield, Sol Strong and Matilda were having babies too, had about ten by the final count. Sarah had five boys, no girls, Charles had six or seven boys, a few girls. Solomon, our brother, never did have any young'uns.

We had Billy, Charlie, Perry, Doug and Clint by the time 1893 came around. We were living pretty good with the new house filling up, fine barn and pasture. I liked being out and driving ol' Dan during the haying, and making a good living driving deliveries for the Tool Shop, up to the depot and back, all around town. Time to time I went to Greenfield with Dan too. Gave me a chance to see Sis and Mother.

Grandmother Judith died back in 1883, a bit after William was born.

Time's when I took the whole kit n'kaboodle from Deerfield back home to Millers with me. Mother'd be sitting up on the seat with me, in back'd be Sarah, couple of her boys along with my two brothers. Driving down through the village, that first time, I could see the neighbors come out on the porch to see us. Before long word got around, gossip mostly about my kinfolk being colored and all. I never gave it much mind. They all knew me anyway. Set up pretty good, friend of Mr. Gunn, I was on the Fire Brigade with the boys, fought the big fire in 1895, so anyway, they kept quiet. Never said anything to my face. Besides I could probably kick the tar out of everybody in town, most of them being maybe five foot six or so, and I'm over six foot, and more with my hat on!

Only, was this one time, some youngster had something to prove. He stopped me while I was out working with Dan and the wagon. Douglass was there with me too. The young man asked me to step down from the wagon, then before you knew it, he knocked my derby hat off. I picked it up, put it back on, and he knocked it off again.

That did it. I told him, "Son, you shouldn't be doing that, you'll get yourself some trouble."

He went and tried to knock it off again, but I caught his arm halfway there and lowered my left fist right on his jaw, almost knocked him over Ol'Dan and the wagon and all. I wasn't going to take that from anybody. Doug had himself a good laugh right then and there. I dare say he never forgot it either. Never did see that bucko again around town, least not around me anyway.

I have to say that when I brought the family through town and down to the house, and when the town gossips got a look at Sarah and her sons, or my brothers Solomon and Charles, that set the tongues a-wagging, not so that I could hear though. I didn't make nothing of it, but with them boys of the Klan stirring up more and more trouble, later it came back on us. Maybe that's why Lizzie got to fussing about Mother and Sarah coming to visit, but I wouldn't stand for her trying to keep them away. Lizzie ran everything, and I'm grateful to her, but kin is kin, and Sister, Mother and I had been through some hard times together, and as long as I had something to say about it, they are welcome here.

Should've known the good luck streak wouldn't last. The 1890s were hard for sure. First, young Charlie got the black diphtheria in November of '93 and t'weren't nothing the doctor could do about it. He took sick and died real fast. Health agents made us bury poor Charlie right away, to stop the spread of the disease. We had to bury him at night, first child up in the new cemetery outside of town. We could see that graveyard from the upstairs window. Lizzie found some solace in that, but her bonnie Charlie was gone. But that wasn't half as bad as when our only girl Ida was taken from us.

It was one of those days in early summer, I can remember as if it was yesterday. Weather was terrible hot and heavy. Nice enough in the morning of that day, on June 26. Haze was rising up along the river, cows lazy in the pasture or standing in the water. Those buzzing locusts started up in the morning, sweet singing larks calling from fence posts in the pasture. School was letting out, last day before vacation, and the boys took their little sister up the street to see their teachers getting ready to close up for the summer. Ida would be going up with the boys for first grade in the fall.

'Bout mid-day, the heat was hard to take. Every chance I got, Dan and I would spend time in the shade, on our way back and forth to the depot.

At noontime, in their rush to get home for dinner, the boys started running down the road from the school, never thinking Ida's little legs couldn't keep up with them, those damn fools. She fell behind, hot and cross, she had quite a temper, she sure was her mother's daughter. By the time the boys figured it out and went back for her, she was on her stomach in the dusty road, crying and turning red. They trucked her home best they could, each one holding arms and legs. She wasn't hard to carry being such a little girl. Lizzie put her on the sofa in the parlor and started wrapping her in wet sheets but that little body was blazing like a stove. Tried some rubbing alcohol, and icy water from the spring.

By the time the Doc came down, she had stopped sweating, but her skin was frightful hot to the touch. She started shaking again, and before long her little soul left her body.

Lizzie stopped the clock, and kept the house dark for a month. It just about broke her heart. We laid our only daughter out right over there in this parlor, between those two windows. We all kept vigil here in the parlor, not wanting her to be alone at night, 'til it was time to put her up on the hill with Charlie.

That was a terrible summer, that one of 1895.

"One less at home!
The charmed circle broken—a dear face
Missed day by day from its usual place
But cleansed, saved, perfected by grace
At home in heaven."

That's what Lizzie wanted on Ida's remembrance card.

We had one more child after that, Alan. He was going to be the one, as is the custom with Lizzie's people, to take care of his mother in her old age. He came along in 1896, and he was the last one for us. Both Lizzie and I were getting up there. I was almost 43 at the time, and although we had a nice piece of land, and I could provide for the whole lot of us, Lizzie wanted no more children. She moved downstairs to the room off the kitchen and I stayed upstairs in the bed by myself. There was no arguing with her, once she decided. No more children.

Will was already fifteen by the time Alan was born, and Alan was to be the last. They were all good sons and Lizzie made sure of that. One by one, they started working at Levi Gunn's Tool Company, same as me.

Turned out Will was pretty musical, played the violin and had a band that played for dances all around here. By the time he got married, he was managing the Dreamland Theater up in Keene where his wife Bessie played piano for the moving pictures. He had a good head for business and that came in handy, because our son Doug was soon going to need a good manager, somebody we could trust.

By the time he was 15, Doug was some ballplayer! Baseball was really catching on, and Doug was one of the best pitchers around, a lefty. Nobody could stop him, nobody could get a hit off him. All our boys played, each one of them in the infield, all brothers. Billy was the manager. Alan was Doug's catcher, Clint played shortstop, and Perry was on third. Just the same, the only ones Lizzie would let practice on Sunday were Alan and Doug. She was a strict Calvinist, but she had a soft spot for baseball and she thought Doug would make something of himself, so she let them practice together outside by the barn, while the rest of us sat in the kitchen reading the Sabbath Bible, or the Almanac.

Doug was so good in high school that a professional team, the Boston Red Sox, came out to have a look at him. They liked what they saw and decided to hire him on the spot. So when he was eighteen, he was pitching in the new ballpark in Boston, the Fenway, in front of a couple thousand people. That was in 1912. Seemed like he was pretty much on his way, getting two hundred dollars a year even, just to play baseball.

He didn't stick with Boston though. There were some dark dealings that happened. I figure it had something to do with my kin. Far as we can make out, some mean-spirited fella from Greenfield wrote the Boston management that Doug wasn't really white. Had black blood. To look at him, you'd never guess that. But back then, some rumor starts and you've got big trouble. Boston had a lily white team, didn't want no blacks or Indians, or mixed bloods. No coloreds on the same team as the white boys. Judging by the likes of who was on the team in those days, couple of Texas boys with Klan connections and all, plus the separation around the country that was going on, no mixing the races, the stories somebody spread about Doug got them all worked up. They probably sent out a spy, some weasel to snoop around town. From what I figure, the snoop took one look at my sister Sarah, or my brothers, and that did it! Back he skedaddled to Boston .

Come March 1913 one month Doug was talking with the reporters about spring training, next month the papers are saying he come down with a heart ailment. That was a lie, nothing wrong with him. Back home he came, sore as hell about it.

He decided he was going to keep on playing ball just the same, but he never went back to Boston. He managed to pitch three innings there in 1912 and that was it. I tell you, we all took to being Red Sox haters after that! Lizzie took it almost harder than Doug. She always figured Sarah, Solomon and Charles, my own brothers and sister, would wind up causing us problems. She never did allow them anywhere near here again. I couldn't face her down, but I was plenty mad.

She got her way, but I went over to Greenfield by myself to see them from time to time. I could take the trolley from upstreet, or take the horse. But it was easier on me and the horse, if I took the trolley. In those days I was sixty-five, pushing seventy. I had a ways to go yet, and I was getting to be an uncle and grandfather couple of times over. Billy, Alan, Perry and Clint all had quite a few children. Doug never did have any. Sarah had five boys, Charles had eight, last one of his was Solomon born in 1909. I was glad he was named for my own uncle Solomon Strong, or maybe for his father's brother Solomon. Either way it's a good name. People like us kept those old names going.

Either way, something'd changed around here. Changed in the country, even in the family. Dividing folks again into black and white, one or the other. I guess once I crossed the river to come here to work at Gunn's factory, I was leaving my colored kinfolk behind, even though I didn't know it at the time.

Didn't realize it then, but my boys were not going to get to know their own kin, my own family, Sarah, Solomon, and Charles. Lizzie wanted to bring them up white. Suppose she was right, the whole country was going that way. If you wanted to get ahead, you better be white. So the family circle we used to have between my kin and me, all back through the Masons and the Jeffreys, was pretty much broken. That door to them pretty much shut. Wasn't really Lizzie's fault, that's the way everything was going. Doug's future ruined because of my colored kin was the last straw for her. She was going to make sure that wouldn't happen again.

So I had lived out my time here, making it to 1929. Mother was gone long before, in 1897, Sarah kept going right up to 1945.

I guess my best years were over long before 1929. But I did have my own children, and grandchildren, the little girls were real pretty. Had my house, had my cat, had Lizzie, and had my fiddle."

He was eyeing the familiar fiddle on the hook in the parlor. I had hung it up there in its usual spot after playing out the night before. Still dusty with rosin, it had a smoky voice, old and mellow after more than one hundred and forty years of playing, coming down through the ages. He took it down from the wall, plucked at it a bit and starting sawing away with the bow held halfway up the wood. He sat perched on the edge of his chair, all long-legged, all knees and elbows. His massive teamster's hand held the slender neck of the fiddle, his fist barely moving, fingers dancing over the strings while the other hand guided the bow to draw forth the tunes. He fiddled merry as a cricket, he scratched out the Hull's Victory, and the Chorus Jig.

When he finished, the tunes still danced in our heads. That sad tale of loss and severance faded, replaced by the merry music of an ancient man visiting from another time.

"Next time, I'll do the 'Preacher and the Bear', *he chuckled.* 'But for now, my time is up. But I'll be around. Just keep me in mind.'

Judah had stopped, withdrawing into his thoughts. Next to him, his sister Sarah sat silently, staring into the room, into the corners where shadows flickered, her eyes shining both sad and dancing. A line from a poet I had just read came to me, without thinking.

"I am the owl's shadow,
a secret member of your family"

Sarah Sharpe Barnes, Judah's sister, then began to speak.

"Guess it's my turn. There's not much to tell, it all seems to have gone by so fast in spite of my almost 90 years. Crow calling in the morning from far over the water, lightning in a summer cloud, oil lamp in the parlor, and a kind of dream.

Seems I've been here all along too. Judah and me, we were always inseparable, as close as brother and sister could be, at least in spirit. But before long, all of our kin forgot our connection, at least the young ones. Nobody ever told them, didn't want to. We kind of had to go our separate ways, things being what they are, or what they became, after a spell. Have to say though, our fortunes sure turned the day Jude and I went to work for Mr. Gunn. Lucky for me I stayed in school down in Connecticut. I learned to read and write, and I could hold my own in the Gunn household. I say our fortunes changed because Judah and I both married within a month of one another, that set us off on different paths even though we both married white people. Like he told you, he headed off over the hill to Millers where there was work. Me, I stayed on with the Gunns for awhile after I married William Barnes in 1881. Will was a good man. He had been in the War of Rebellion and got wounded pretty bad, almost right off. That was a strange twist, 'cause later on that war pension kept me going me going for almost fifty years afterward.

We had some good times, and we had five boys, Frank, Herbert, William, Royal, and Harold, all big and strong. Even if William was white, our boys were still considered colored, even fought in the colored regiments in the Great War. Will worked on the railroad for awhile, best he could what with his wound from the war. By and by he found out how to get that invalid's pension, so that helped us out quite a bit.

Way back, he started out boarding with my mother down in Deerfield, that's how we got to know each other. He was close to ten years older than me, and had been married once already, but for some reason, we hit it off, in spite of all. He started courting me, and pretty soon we figured we should get married. You couldn't tell by looking at me now, but I was pretty good looking then, if I do say so myself. In those days, color didn't matter all that much, just a little, and after the War it was easier for the colors to mix. That didn't last long though, by the time we were married five or six years, things got back to being rough for us.

My mother Betsy moved in with us as she started failing, even though she wasn't very old, her health stayed bad, and got worse. Will died about ten years after Mother, in 1909. Lucky for me the war widow's pension kept coming in right up to 1945. The boys were getting good jobs as machinists and such, at the Tap and Die factory. They helped me out as best they could.

Like I said, Judah and I drifted away from each other even though only a few miles were between us. He did come over to fetch me, Mother, and the boys to go over to Millers once or twice a year, but after Mother died in 1897, then that baseball problem in 1913, something changed, and he didn't invite us anymore. I think he sort of wanted to, but times were changing, and 'course both of us had our hands full with big families. He came over to Greenfield for things like weddings and funerals, but before long, I could tell that his boys were growing up without knowing anything about their Aunt Sarah. Not anything about Charles or Solomon either. Before long, it was like we didn't exist.

Then my side of the family decided to forget about *them* too.

I moved around a lot after Will died, but finally settled in over on Lincoln Street, and I was pretty comfortable. My son Herbert lived next door. I kept up my reading, and even wrote a few poems from time to time that some people liked.

That's all there is to tell. I kept to myself, and took care of my sons and their children, even their children's children. That's a blessing. My sons all married into good families in town, and I had visitors all the time. Can't ask for much more, and I didn't. The older I got, and I got real old, the more comfort reading and writing were for me. Thank God I had that. I thought about my brother a lot when I could, I do wish we could've stayed closer. We went through a lot in the old days. But that was the way of the world.

Guess I really was the dark shadow of his family, but we can't say I'm the *secret* member of the family anymore, can we?"

She left us with a wink and a wry smile, as well as a growing sense that what had been broken was getting mended, bit by bit, one secret at a time.

Just then, it became clear that there was a small form fidgeting just beyond the lamplight. Trim and thin-lipped, her hair drawn back tight in a bun, the small lady looked, even glared at us through wire frame glasses and sharp eyes.

I guessed in a second we were in for it. Everything about this lady was prim and tight, self-assured and righteous. Her sober-colored dress buttoned up right around her neck, this little woman taut with controlled energy was going to have her say, and no one was going to stop Lizzie Moir Smith.

"Well you don't have to guess my name, do you. And isn't that myself sitting up there in the portrait on the wall, so even if some of you are slow, you can put two and two together! And you know why I'm here.

Her gaze softened, as she looked all of us over. She was not going to make a scene.

"This is my house too, don't forget. My children were born here, and you know how some died here. This room was a place of joy and, Lord help us, a place of many a sorrow. But this house is still here and you're still in it, mostly thanks to me, so don't you be forgetting that fact, while you're going on about how unfair life can be. Of course Jude had a role in providing this house too, so you can all thank him for some of what you've got now. While you're at it, you can thank him *and* me.

I'm telling you now that that you can well think what you want about me, but I kept this family on the straight and narrow, gave them what they needed for values in life, gave them a good Scots backbone, and none of them went astray. They had good strong Christian values which is more than I can say for the likes of some of you here. My boys turned out fine, and even Mr. Smith here, in spite of his family of coloreds, he went on to his final reward with a clear conscience and a clean soul.

But it wasn't easy. It was never easy. How I wound up here, I can hardly understand or even believe it. We don't know why the Lord put us here to go through so many travails. But it isn't our lot to ask questions. I had to leave my brothers and sisters when I was still a young lass, and though it was damp and always gray back home, I never stopped missing it. I can't help missing that purple heather in the uplands, even to this day. I was never to return, never gaze on Aberdeen, nor on any of my family again.

None of you know what that's like, to live in a foreign land, to leave your home and family and start all over from scratch. I can't say whether I ever did feel at home here, even after fifty years of trying to understand this country.

Things were rough and wild here when I came over and down from Nova Scotia to work for Captain O'Keefe. It was really dangerous and uncivilized in those days even compared to my Scotland. Lucky for me I had a cousin or two in Greenfield, and the Church provided great comfort in the Lord, and gave me strength to hold out against the likes of the people I found in this place.

I have to admit of course, that I took a great fondness for Jude, and we were grand with each other. Such a big man, it took a lot to keep him in line, and tame him down a bit but in his heart he knew I was right for him, and it was best for his own good. He needed a strong Christian woman like me, coming from where he did. When I took and accepted him, I took his family along with him, for better or worse. He was a handsome man with some good qualities about him, and I could've done worse. But it took a lot of patience, and God gave me the will to face all that I endured.

I should have known that his family would create problems for me sooner or later. They did things in a different way, and they were just too dark-skinned for me. Especially the way the country was going by 1900. We were trying to get ahead, and it was really a hindrance to have colored blood in the family.

I did put up with it. I did unto others as I would have others do unto me. But I preferred to keep *them* at a safe distance. I cannot say they were bad people, just different I suppose. I was glad when we moved away a few miles where it would be easier to make a life for ourselves and our boys, and get on with living as a good Christian white family.

Even though I tried, I couldn't keep the dark blood of the family from coming out. People knew about Judah, since his mother, brothers, and sisters often visited us here, but neighbors were always decent with us in spite of it. We kept up appearances, owned more land in town than most families, and I made sure we bought more whenever there was a chance. You must never separate from your land. You must never sell it, it's the only treasure you'll ever be sure of, along with God's love. So we had good standing in this village. Jude and I were respected.

It came to be though, that people were thinking more and more that the races ought to be kept separate. I had to agree with them, no good would come of the colors associating with one another.

It all came to a head when Douglass lost his best chance at getting out into the world, his best chance to make good money at playing professional ball with that Red Sox team, and rising up in society. Jude's family ruined it for him and that was the last straw. I wasn't going to tolerate them coming around any more, I wasn't going to let anybody else in the family suffer the humiliation like Douglass and I did.

And that's the whole of it. None of them were bad people, they were just too dark, and I had to do something about it, for my sons and for the rest of the family. Couldn't get anywhere, couldn't get ahead with dark skin, the whole country knew that, including red, white, and black people. I was no different from anybody else in the country. I was bound and determined that our boys would be raised *white*, and no one was to mention the coloreds from across the river, ever again. I suppose it was tough on Judah, but I had left all my family behind too, on the other side of the ocean.

Now you can say what you will, but I know I'm right. I didn't want to know those people anymore, and I made sure the rest of the family forgot them. I had to do right by the family, and I did. It was the only way to get ahead.

But forgiveness is Christian, and I will say to you Betsy, to you Judah, and to you Sarah, that I meant you no personal harm. And I hope that you will forgive me as I forgive you, the whole lot of you down the ages and generations. I just did what I had to do.

Betsy H. Strong – Alan C. Smith

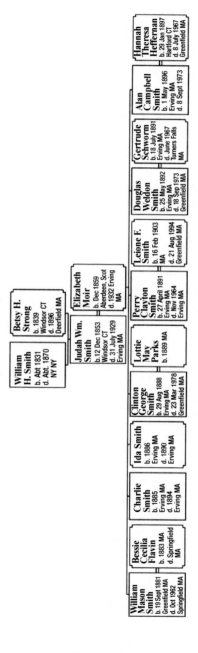

Chapter 10

The Gungy 2009

Like most aspects of this genealogical adventure, stray pieces of the puzzle turned up in unexpected places, at unexpected times, and yet fit perfectly into the mosaic that forms the whole.

I was sleepless in Paris, having arrived earlier the day before, pausing there on the way to our annual visit to family in Brittany. The difference in time zones between the East Coast of New England and the Continent had me up and sleepily poking away at the laptop in the dark kitchen, under the reading lamp, at 4 AM.

I had put off googling the Historical Society of East Lyme for a while now, with so many other projects to pursue. But this was as good a time as any, since I was in a somewhat forced state of inactivity.

East Lyme played a very important role in the family's history, and I knew that we were bound to go to there sooner or later, to pick up the trail of Joseph Jeffrey's son, grandson, and extended family members who relocated to Nehantic lands on Black Point. They had returned to these ancestral lands in Lyme as the Ninigrets and allied families, including the Jeffreys, fell under more and more challenges from the Anti-Sachem Party in Charlestown, Rhode Island, circa 1740.

Quickly, the East Lyme Historical Society webpage popped up. I clicked on events, to see what they were up to.

In an instant, I was wide awake. One week hence, an anthropologist from Lyme, one Dr. John Pfeiffer, was to give a talk to the Society entitled: "The Nehantics, Where Are They Now?"

Merde! (My French was coming back fast!) I'd miss it! There's no way I could get back for that talk, I'd just landed in Paris!

I shot off a message to the secretary of the Society, and within a day she had sent me Dr. Pfeiffer's phone number in Lyme. It would have to wait. We were in France for a month, but contacting him would be at the top of the list when I got back. The ancestors do work in mysterious ways, even in the electronic era!

Once back in Massachusetts a month later, I had Dr. Pfeiffer on the phone. I had had to leave a voicemail stating that I was a descendant of the Jeffrey family of Charlestown and East Lyme, and that my family and I had been tracking George Jeffrey Sr. and George Jeffrey Jr. to Connecticut. I left that message, adding that we'd love to talk to him. Within two minutes Dr. John called back, full of questions and eager to talk to someone with Lyme tribal connections.

I told him of the plans my cousin Donald Scott and I had to journey to Lyme within a week, and he offered to meet us in the town of Niantic, at the site called Black Point. I'd had Black Point and a hunting tract called the Gungy on my mind, after having heard it mentioned by Rebecca Jeffrey, and in subsequent readings. These sites were extremely important in family oral history, for they were at the heart of the Nehantic people and their reservation. The Jeffrey family had a long history at both the Black Point reserve as well as on the Gungy Tract, after they had left the Narragansett Reservation in Rhode Island. We needed to find these places, to get a feel for them, to find what spirits remained there.

When we were ready to go there, this man appeared. We had our guide.

We set out from our Valley that morning filled with the excitement and high expectations for a promising road trip on the trail of the ancestors. We would not be disappointed.

We found McCook Park at the base of Black Point. Niantic Bay was within a few hundred yards from where we waited for John Pfeiffer. The entire sector was highly developed, every inch occupied by summer homes, year-round residences, and fenced in yards. We left the car in the shade of an oak and got out to stretch our legs. The temperature was hovering near 95 degrees.

Within fifteen minutes, John Pfeiffer arrived.

He stepped out of a battered Land Rover-style 4x4, wearing faded baseball cap, shorts, tee-shirt and holding what was to prove an ever-present cup of coffee. His handshake was firm, fingers gnarled and worn from digging anthropological treasures, I figured. Here was an Indiana Jones for our generation.

He began quickly telling us the story of our ancestral lands, of our people, of Lyme, and of ourselves. Donald and I listened intently so as not to miss a word. But the information was flowing fast. We were enthralled, trying to remember it all. The flow of words and information was to last all day, more than seven hours!

Fairly quickly we realized he needed to share some secrets about this land. He had been waiting a long time for some Nehantic descendants to appear.

The most startling revelation concerned the stretch of land before us, and the street just opposite from where we were standing. The hairs on the back of my neck stood on edge, the anger rose up as he spoke of the injustice suffered by the local tribe at the hands of the overseers and the state legislature.

We knew, and Rebecca Jeffrey had told us long before, that the few Nehantics remaining on the Black Point reservation had accepted to relinquish their rights to the land there. Their conditions for turning over the land had been simple: the money the tribe was owed for the sale of the remaining tribal lands was to be used to protect the Indian burial ground *in perpetuity*.

We stood looking at the place where that burial ground should have been. However, all we could see over the graves was a residential street, lined with fenced-in yards, lawn ornaments, and American flagpoles. John explained sarcastically that "perpetuity" didn't last long, after all.

He told us that in the 1880s when a developer had decided to build a grand hotel on the rise behind us, looking out over Black Point and the bay, he didn't want the gaze of his wealthy guests settling on some old Indian cemetery directly in the foreground of the panoramic view. The authorities apparently complied with his request to do something about that. They removed the stones marking a few graves, along with a few bones, and posited them in a corner of the Union cemetery overlooking a creek. Of all those buried there on Black Point over the last 500 years, only five or six graves were removed.

The open space was created by the developer for the benefit of his wealthy tourists, but that didn't last long either. Soon building lots were surveyed and made available for cottages. But curiously, any building permits granted had stipulated that there could be no cellar excavations, nor holes dug in any of the lots, and with good reason! There were 500 years of Indian graves just below the surface.

We all gazed at the houses neatly aligned on the street. We began to realize that it was likely that George Jeffrey and many of his extended family were buried under these homes, for he had owned several acres on the Point, had lived and died here, along with other Nehantic and mixed-blood farmers.

As the realization that my ancestors lay beneath these lawns, beneath the garden gnomes, plastic pink flamingos and flagpoles, the anger rose within. For years now, John himself has been appalled by the injustices perpetrated in the name of his own hometown over a century ago. He had discovered this ugly truth quite by accident more than 15 years back. He had published his findings, in collaboration with one Donald Malcarne in 1989. In his investigation, he hoped to "raise questions… about the cemetery that are not only historical and archaeological, but social, economic, ideological, moral, and legal."

Now, with Donald and me on the site with him, he was able to pass on this information to the descendants of those buried there.

We had another site to visit. We had heard of the Gungy Tract, hundreds of acres set aside for the Nehantics where they could hunt, farm, and cut firewood and lumber.

We piled into the car and covered the ten miles away from the coast, into the interior, through rolling farmlands and woodlands, John talking all the while. Recently retired from teaching like myself, he could now turn his attention to the homelands of the Nehantics full time. He had spent a lifetime of work fitting together the anthropologies and cultures of his hometown and, with our arrival on the scene, several strands of the mysteries were converging.

As we approached the Tract, we turned off the forest road into a small clearing and left the car. Just beyond was a wide padlocked gate barring a footpath that led into the Gungy. Such a strange name, its meaning lost in time. John's thinking is that the Tract had been left to people who lived on the margins of the society of the 1700s. Here, Blacks, Indians and poor Whites could scratch out an existence on this undesirable land.

John told us how the Tract had been saved from development just recently. The current landowner had been bound and determined to develop the Tract as multi-use recreational destination, but John and a number of like-minded citizens had talked him out of it. It has now been preserved in its historic state, with an extensive trail system that was designed primarily by John and his mother, who had always hiked this area together since John had learned to walk.

Into the Tract we went, and quickly we found ourselves scrambling over the ruins of a sawmill. John speculated that it was likely that George Jeffrey Sr. and George Jeffrey Jr. had participated in the building and running of this mill, since we could place both of them on the site when it was operational. And given the fact that the Charlestown, Rhode Island sawmill had been run by Joseph Jeffrey for years, it's likely that sawyering ran in the family.

Trails wound up and over ledges and outcrops, through small wooded glens once cleared by whites and Indians alike to farm along the quiet streams there. Eventually, deep into the Tract, he pointed out the foundation of a farmstead whose owner had been identified, and whose land had abutted the Jeffreys' holdings, but he couldn't be quite sure where the Jeffrey place had actually been.

Up on a small wooded hilltop, John showed us the ruins of stone fortifications and sites built under John Winthrop, Jr. in the 1630s to provide a refuge and a home for the Puritans if a turn of events in England placed them in danger of invasion. Their enemies never came.

We finished the hike near the foundations of a massive barn, abandoned in the 1850s by men and families who headed west, getting away from the rocky, exhausted terrain here.

We paused for a commemorative picture as we came out of the Tract.

John remarked:

"I wouldn't be surprised, when you print that picture, that you'll see a long line of people standing behind the three of us."

We knew what he meant. We could feel the presence of those who had come here before us. They were there, all around us, welcoming me and Donald back.

John Pfeiffer had one more gift for us. In the land records of Lyme, he had found the deeds to property on Black Point dating from 1782 when George Jeffrey Jr. had purchased land from Sarah Jeffrey, his sister. George Sr. had left parcels of his land holdings to all of his children. They were then bought out by George Jr. The deeds covered a period between 1782 and 1784, and contained names, signatures, and marks that had become very familiar to us over the years: Widow Eunice Jeffrey, Jack Nebo and George's sister Phebe (Jeffrey) Nebo, Phillip Occuish, and of course George Jeffrey himself.

"These are your people." John said. "It's your family."

We didn't know how to thank him. He had taken the time to research and copy those deeds linking us to the names on the document, placing us here on our ancient homelands. He had given us a priceless gift. Deflecting our words of gratefulness, he added:

"Well, I owe a lot to the Nehantics. Now that I've brought you here, the circle is complete. I've done my job, now I can rest easy."

"Maybe so," I said to myself. "But I have a feeling we're just getting started."

And for sure, we all knew that there is rarely an end to the searching. But for the rest of the journey in this part of Connecticut, we had found our guide.

Chapter 11

Pete (1917-1986)

Silence in the parlor, dusk deepening outside the windows. The panes of old fashioned window glass cause ripples in the forms of the trees and in the darkening woods at the edge of the autumn yard. Inside, the cast iron stove ticks, the oak burning in the firebox shifts and glows. The oil lamp still burns its yellow light, throwing shadows on the wall, deepening and darkening the features of all of us sitting there, staring into the silence, words of our last visitors occupying our thoughts. This is to be the final gathering; we will have all spoken by the time the evening has ended.

Slowly the awareness of a form defining itself at the small round table near the stove, just outside the circle of light thrown by the lamp. Of course. She'd choose that spot, always her favorite when visiting over the years. She sat still, looking out the window with those melancholy eyes. I remembered how she often half smiled when we saw the great blue heron winging up the river, the mass of the mountain heaving up behind in the western light. That heron meant something to her; she always sighed when she saw it. She believed in omens.

This was the woman who managed to keep the story of the family's history. They say there's always at least one in each generation and she was the one. And that day long ago, she decided maybe I was the one, maybe not, but back in the den in 1973, she had told me the secret, the story of the portrait. And that had started this process, this journey of pushing back the deliberate darkness that shrouded our family's origins. What she had told me over the remaining few years of her life, gradually took on meaning thirty years later, and the family story began reclaiming its shape after years of denial and deliberate neglect. Her first-hand accounts and remembrance gave perspective, depth, and life to the names and dates we uncovered.

Tonight though, fittingly, she was to be our last visitor. As always she had the faraway look that inner sadness and weariness impart. Eyes that rarely smiled, head held at a thoughtful angle, strong angular facial features, yet she had that clear look of a streak of toughness and defiance, as if she were still thumbing her nose at the inevitability of life's tragedy.

While she was living, and visiting me, mutual enjoyment of family memories and glasses of whiskey always joined us, she and I. Couldn't offer her that now, nor could I hold out a cigarette for her. Tobacco had killed her, I couldn't offer her a smoke, besides there wasn't a cigarette in the house. She smiled her thin-lipped half smile, and began.

"There's not much I can tell you that you don't already know. You've already found out more than I ever knew anyway. Of course I went against what the others wanted when I told you about Judah and his family connections, and the hidden side, the dark side of the family. But I'm glad I did. Gave you something to think about, didn't it?

You already know about me. Born in 1917, I was the first one born to Abe and Hannah. They named me Elizabeth after my grandmother Elizabeth Moir. She and I later became very close. Right off I should've known that'd be a bad luck name, but I didn't have anything to say about it at the time, that's for sure. Later they nicknamed me Pete, probably because they wanted a boy, and I wound up being such a tomboy anyway.

And brother you better believe it, I never took any guff from anybody. I'd fight if I had to, we all would. I could never stand anyone thinking they were better than us, even if we *were* poor.

When we were kids, the family moved around a lot. We lived all over town, up on Pleasant Street, over across the Flat, all over. Then when Grandfather Judah died, we moved in here with my grandmother Elizabeth. She came over from Scotland as a young girl. Poor woman. Later on she'd sit with me over there at the kitchen table and look out at the yard, all full of mud and manure. She'd put her elbow on the table, her chin in her palm and fingers on the side of her head, and she'd ask over and over "How did I wind up *here*?"

She used to talk about working for the Queen at Balmoral Castle near Aberdeen where all the Moirs come from. She kept pictures of the castle in a drawer upstairs. She was a tiny little thing but tough as nails. Calvinist too, and she ran this place with an iron hand. And Judah was such a big galoot, I don't know how she did it. Seven children, all boys, except for Ida their little girl who died of heat stroke, running back from school on a hot day.

Grandmother's the one who told me about Judah working for Levi Gunn. She said his family came from down south. Funny how later you learned that "down south" was actually the south of Connecticut, not below the Mason-Dixon Line like we all thought!

He drove Levi Gunn's carriage around Greenfield for him. She told me how we were related to some black families from over on Deerfield Street. There was the Harris family, and the Barnes family. She even told me the name of Herbert Barnes, but that's all I remember. I was only about 10 years old at the time. I think you've found out now that Herbert was Judah's nephew, son of his sister Sarah. I didn't know anything about her.

I never felt comfortable around Judah. He was rough, always pinching me and teasing. I never put up with him that much. I talked back quite a bit, and I stayed away from him. It made him laugh to see how mad I got at him.

He had a goatee and always wore a bowler hat. Really tall, big hands. He sure could play the fiddle though. He used to sit over there in the parlor near the piano. He'd sit up on the edge of the chair, big as life and play away. People liked him to do "The Preacher and the Bear". We'd all laugh like hell when he came to "Lord, please don't help that BEAR!"

Knowing what Grandmother told me, I'd look hard to see if I could find any black in him, but I couldn't tell. He probably was the reason Doug Smith got kicked off the Red Sox. Somebody from Greenfield snitched on him. Said he was part black. The story went around saying that it was appendicitis or a heart condition, but everybody in town knew they got rid of him because he had black blood. My grandmother Elizabeth sure felt it was like a curse. The whole town knew of course. There was so much gossip.

When I was growing up, some of the tougher kids from upstreet would call us names I won't repeat here. But they all meant that we weren't white, more like only part white, not as good as them. That's when my temper would get up and I'd say things back that maybe I'd be sorry for. But I just wouldn't take it from the likes of them, thinking they were better than us. That's when a fight would start and the fists would fly. I could throw a good punch and they knew it! Those fights didn't last long, but it's sure as shoot nobody was going to give me and my family any crap without getting a good belt from me!

Times weren't easy. Jesus! I can remember during the Depression my mother getting a letter from her Aunt Johannah over in Ireland asking if we could send her any cast-off clothes for the family back in Killorglin. For God's sake, we were so poor we didn't have a pot to piss in or a window to throw it out of! But at least my father had a job at the Tool Shop, all through that time. Mr. Gunn made sure all the Smith family had work there if they wanted. Plus we always had a pig, a horse, a couple of cows and chickens. Grew our own vegetables down below in the pasture so we weren't starving, that's for sure. Lots of times, we fed other kids just to help them out.

I got married twice, the first time I was pretty young. We had a son we called Pat. I got a divorce after a few years. We just didn't get along. When we divorced, my ex was pretty bitter. Said he was glad to get rid of me, he called me names, said we were just a bunch of niggers anyway. He was from Greenfield so he probably knew about the family connections. Just the same he didn't have to say that, what a mean thing to say, that Son of a B.

Second time I got married, I stayed married. Johnny and I had five children, but we lost three of them too early in their lives. It's awful to bury your own children, to keep living well past the time they're gone. They had Cystic, of all the rotten luck, Johnny and I were carriers. Two of our boys, Jim and Tom, didn't have it and stayed healthy. But I lost Pat though when he got shot out hunting bears. Blown away. Live by the gun and die by the gun I guess. That's the whole of it.

We had a few good times now and then, but it still seems like it was one damn thing after another.

Funny how sometimes I think about a little colored girl who was often visiting across the street. God she was cute, big eyes and beautiful skin. She came over to visit from Greenfield. Don't know why, but I always felt we were connected somehow. They say there's some instinct in you that helps you to recognize your kin, even if you never saw them before. Guess I'll never know, but it sure felt like there was something there between us.

Looking back, I have to say I was glad back then when I could tell as much of the family story as I knew, even if the rest of them didn't want me to. It would've been a terrible shame if any of that was lost. Somebody has to remember, somebody has to tell, and somebody has to write it down. Otherwise, what's the use?

If you don't learn about your own people, then you're just another name, just another face, and after you're gone, nobody will know who they were, who *you* were, what you did while you were here, what you had to go through. I knew what I was doing when I told the secret, and I'm glad of it. It's good for you to know who your people were, and are, it tells you something. I'm glad I spilled the beans back in Doug's den that day. It helped keep us going, and it sure kept you busy, that's for damn sure.

I just want to be able to say I was here. I stuck it out, and by Jaysus it wasn't easy. More than once I wanted to take the gas pipe. But nobody can say I ever gave up, but I guess I did have to give in, at the end. Not much was ever going to work out. I did have a gift for taking care of people. I learned how the hard way, but at least I had that.

Don't pay any more attention to me now. I'll just sit here near the window for the next couple of minutes. I like listening to the stories. Glad you remember me, and don't worry about me at all. It's OK, and I'm alright now. I'll be watching that cardinal out there. Sure is pretty. Always liked that red bird."

Betsy H. Strong – Elizabeth "Pete" Smith

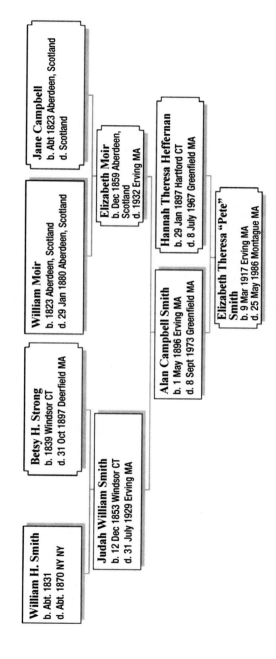

Jane Campbell
b. Abt 1823 Aberdeen, Scotland
d. Scotland

Elizabeth Moir
b. Dec 1859 Aberdeen, Scotland
d. 1932 Erving MA

William Moir
b. 1823 Aberdeen, Scotland
d. 29 Jan 1880 Aberdeen, Scotland

Hannah Theresa Heffernan
b. 29 Jan 1897 Hartford CT
d. 8 July 1967 Greenfield MA

Betsy H. Strong
b. 1839 Windsor CT
d. 31 Oct 1897 Deerfield MA

Alan Campbell Smith
b. 1 May 1896 Erving MA
d. 8 Sept 1973 Greenfield MA

Elizabeth Theresa "Pete" Smith
b. 9 Mar 1917 Erving MA
d. 25 May 1986 Montague MA

Judah William Smith
b. 12 Dec 1853 Windsor CT
d. 31 July 1929 Erving MA

William H. Smith
b. Abt. 1831
d. Abt. 1870 NY NY

Chapter 12

Incident in Hebron 2010

Week by week and month after month the friendship and deeper understanding of family connectedness between Donald and me was growing. We began regular meetings at cousin Barbara's welcoming living room to discuss new discoveries, new connections, to read and revise new chapters and adventures in the unfolding family journey.

Layer by layer we peeled back the years, sometimes methodically, sometimes jumping from one anecdote to another depending on intuition and inspiration. Questions and mysteries remained: Where were the records of Judah's father? Why was Betsy listed as *"Name Cannot Be Known"* ?

Why did racial descriptions on the census vary from black to mulatto to white, often for the same person? I was still wrestling with what I was actually seeking in this process of continual discovery, but it was sure that one aspect of the family story was becoming clearer and clearer: the fateful issue of skin color, and its impacts on our lives over the generations.

Donald and I had clearly a common ancestral lineage: we both descended from a mutual great grandmother, Betsy Strong, who had lived out her life within seven miles of where we both now lived. She was a black woman, or was she? She was Indian, or was she? In one census she was even called white, after being called black ten years before. She died as an "African". What was really going on then, and did it matter?

Whatever the situation, Donald and I are linked by blood, DNA, geography and destiny. Yet we are from culturally different worlds. I was coming to realize that a part of the story I was pursuing, besides trying to unravel the genealogical twists of our mutual family, was the unconscious effort to place our lives side by side to try to discern what different had happened to us.

Did racial difference really shape our lives? Of the four siblings, Judah, Sarah, Solomon, and Charles, only my great grandfather Judah moved into the white world, whereas his three siblings, including Donald's great grandfather, remained in the colored, black, mixed-race world. We were learning how different their life experiences were, and how, as the siblings moved into their later years, their worlds were separated, their worlds became so radically different, so defined by their times, so harshly structured by the sociopolitical imperatives of a racially divided nation.

As the underlying theme of exploring our racially different existences came more into focus, an interesting opportunity for learning something new, plus the possibility of an new family chapter, a new adventure, revealed itself. Donald received an invitation from the Hebron Historical Society in Connecticut to attend a premiere screening of a film based on an incident in Hebron just after the Revolutionary War. The incident involved two maternal ancestors of Donald's: Cesar and Lois Peters. Donald's great-grandmother was Mary Anne Peters of Hebron.

Curiously enough, back at the Fiddlers' Gathering to honor John Putnam, early in this genealogical adventure, we got involved in a conversation with one elderly gentleman by the name of Peters, a member of the interconnected black families attending the reunion of Putnam's descendants. In his late seventies, tall, high cheekbones, ponytail and relaxed manner, we spent time that day talking about both his youth and later his time in the armed services in France. Offhandedly he had mentioned the oral histories handed down in the Peters family: he thought he was descended from slaves who had lived in

Hebron, Connecticut, but he didn't know much more. He also had said that family history linked him to the ill-fated Pequot nation of southern Connecticut.

Barbara had gotten on the trail, sensing a story and a potentially fascinating historical episode. She quickly uncovered the story of Cesar and Lois Peters, and linked this gentleman to his ancestors. The family oral history had proved true. The new discoveries by Barbara however, also linked Donald to both Cesar and Lois through his mother Bernice. The African-American side of our family was quickly taking on added depth and perspective.

The story of Cesar and Lois, best related in the account by Rose and Brown in their book *Tapestry*, published by the New London County Historical Society in 1979, described the Hebron incident which was to be celebrated in a documentary film directed by a young NYU Film School graduate who was born and raised in Hebron.

The basic storyline is summarized as follows:

The Peters couple were what we could call "faithful" slaves of one Reverend Samuel Peters of Hebron, just before, and during, the Revolutionary War. Peters himself, the slaveholder, was a Tory and very much against the men who called themselves Patriots and who were partisans in the revolt against the King. As the Revolutionary War evolved, the pressure grew on all the Tories in New England, and like many other Loyalists, Rev. Peters fled to England. But before leaving the country, he promised Cesar, Lois, and their children their freedom as long as they looked after the house and property he was leaving behind. So Cesar, Lois, and their five children lived in the Peters house during the war years, grateful to be earning their freedom.

However, while he was in England, Peters fell into debt and went back on his word. He sold Cesar, Lois, and children to a slaveholder, one David Prior from South Carolina, in 1787. This man was determined to travel up to Connecticut to claim his newly acquired slaves and bring them back to his plantation in the south. He arrived by ship at the port of New Haven and made his way up to Hebron.

Cesar and his family had been well integrated into Hebron society for years and were highly respected as true members of the community. The townspeople would certainly have challenged the slave-holder over his intentions of making off with the black family but for the fact that all the able-bodied men were away from town that day, drilling with the militia . So they were unaware that Cesar and his family were being trundled up into a wagon for the journey to the ship waiting in New Haven and ready to sail for the South.

According to reports, Cesar tried to resist, but under threats of the slaver's posse he had to gather up the family's belongings and get into the wagon for the journey to the port. They shed many tears along the way and tried every ruse they could think of to slow the wagon down, including trying to add what stones they found along the way to make the wagon heavier.

When the Hebron militiamen returned and heard what had happened, they set out in hot pursuit, arriving at the dockside just as the ship was making ready to sail. The slaveholder posed a dilemma however, showing the townspeople a bill of sale for the black family. But the Hebron men had worked up a contingency plan. One Elijah Graves, the Hebron tailor, claimed that Cesar was making off with clothing he had not yet paid for, and that prompted the officer of the militia to arrest Cesar on the spot, to be brought back for trial to Hebron, to answer for the crime of stealing clothing.

The details of the supposed crime of course were slightly different. Cesar had indeed ordered a waistcoat and breeches from the Hebron tailor, on credit, as was the custom of the time. He had agreed to pay off the debt of the cost of the clothing by working for the tailor, bartering his labor for the clothing. The problem was that the debt hadn't yet been worked off, and Casar had left town, and therefore he was in legal trouble and should be arrested.

The slave-holder, not only having been outwitted by some Yankee ingenuity, but also being quite outnumbered by the armed militia, acquiesced, and the black family headed back to Hebron.

A trial ensued, in which Cesar was found guilty of absconding without paying his debt. He was ordered to remain in Hebron indefinitely while he worked off his debt as he had initially agreed. Arrangements were made so that the debt of labor would take a really long time indeed.

The crux of the trial however, hinged on the testimony of Elijah Graves, who had to testify under oath that in fact the clothes in question were indeed "stolen" by Cesar. The black man's fate, as well as that of his family, depended on Graves, as he wrestled with his conscience. Would he swear that the clothing was stolen or would he falter by testifying that perhaps all of this was just a ruse, or a case of an uncertain memory? The pressures were tremendous for an ill-educated man of strong principle. At that time a man's word often times was his most cherished possession.

In fact, he did testify that the clothing was stolen, and the slaver went back to South Carolina empty-handed. Cesar and his family remained in Hebron for the rest of their lives, living in the Tory Peters' house.

This story was just asking to be recounted on film. So the afore-mentioned native son of Hebron, a budding cinematographer, chose the subject as his thesis project for his degree in film. The invitation to attend the screening arrived at Donald's home, and we were determined to go to the ceremony at the premiere.

Donald was inspired by the convergence of circumstances involving his ancestor, and he began preparing what he would say at the ceremony, and he asked me to go with him. The three of us headed south to Hebron that day, Donald, his son Shannon, and me.

The car that day of course was full of talk. We didn't often have Shannon with us on these genealogical excursions, so we spent a lot of the time getting him caught up with Barbara's latest discoveries and our latest efforts at connecting the dots. We were on a beeline to Hebron.

Soon enough, we found the high school where the screening was to take place. A magnificent modern building, it looked more like a university than a public high school. We concluded that Hebron had to be one rich community indeed.

We approached the reception table of the Hebron Historical Society, where Donald and Shannon introduced themselves as descendants of Cesar and Lois Peters and that they had been contacted about attending. We were told that surely there was a section where the Peters descendants were seated.

First disappointment. Nothing was organized for the Peters family. We found three seats off to the side of the auditorium and waited for things to happen. I did find the Chairwoman of the Historical Society to tell her we were there, and knowing that Vickie Welch, a published, professional genealogist who had done a lot of research on the Jeffrey family of the Nehantic/Narragansetts was somewhere in the hall. I asked the

Chairwoman that she let Vickie know that we were looking for her. Welch had been crucial in our genealogical research. Her massive book *And They Were Related To...* was a treasure trove of information about the Jeffery family, and numerous related families of color throughout southern New England. She was also instrumental in preserving the Peters home in Hebron, and thus saving it from destruction. Unfortunately, we were not to meet that day.

Presently, the writer/director arrived on stage. Young, fresh, intelligent, he received an enthusiastic reception from the audience. It began to dawn on me that this was a favorite son from Hebron, a recent graduate of this very high school, and before long it became clear that this event was really about *him*.

The film was an excellent 50-minute docudrama, well directed and produced with local actors and townspeople playing the key roles in the story. The black actors however had next to no speaking roles and basically filled the space that should have evoked something of the character and spirit of the black family. Another disappointment.

The drama of the film in fact focused on the struggle of conscience of one white man, Elijah Graves, who held the Peters family's fate (and the destiny of their descendant Donald) in his hands. The trial on film reached its foregone conclusion. The Peters family stayed in Hebron, and the slaver, infuriated, returned home to the South empty-handed.

The house lights came on to thunderous applause, the three of us sat in silence and looked at one another. Donald shrugged. The youthful director appeared on stage, buoyed by the reception, and like any Academy Award winner, began the litany of thanks to Those Who Made It Possible. The actors stood up together and were applauded, black and white. The film crew, the editors, the family of the director were all acknowledged. He said his final thanks and prepared to leave the stage. We exchanged more dubious, or rather, dismayed looks. Then he changed his exit path, returned center stage saying he needed one more opportunity to extends his thanks to...

...his MOTHER! More wild applause, which shortly faded. Good boy, he remembered to thank his mom. Then a black woman's strong voice bellowed from the audience:

"What about the Peters family? We all traveled here for this, what about US?" The young director asked the family's descendants to stand, but to our dismay the whole hall rose in a standing ovation, submerging the Peters family in the anonymity of the crowd - the crowd having effectively made them disappear.

The hall emptied, and we were left standing there still looking at one another, shaking our heads and wondering what had just happened. We drove all the way for this? We had anticipated this event for weeks and it came to THIS? Sure, the film was technically well done, the acting solid, the crisis of conscience well portrayed. But it was all one-dimensional. Cesar and Lois remained background figures, their personalities barely sketched, their fearful, later thankful, expressions stereotyping the image of blacks as viewed by whites. The film fell into a fateful trap of helping whites feel good about themselves for helping black folks.

Undeterred, and ever so slightly masking his frustration at not being able to express what he had been preparing to share as a descendant of Cesar and Lois, Donald strode up the aisle and out into the lobby, his scroll of the family tree in his fist, determined to take matters into his own hands.

I scouted up and down the lobby hall, expecting a reception ceremony, a gathering of people, a chance to meet the young director. Nothing organized came into sight, at least nothing we were invited to. Clusters of whites discussed sociably, separate groups of blacks chatted. Donald, with Shannon and me close behind, approached an elderly black gentleman, introduced himself, shared his background and relationship with Cesar and Lois, and the connection was made.

Before long more and more descendants of the Peters gathered around and the impromptu family reunion began. Shannon warmed to the discussion; I was blended in easily, without reservations. Shannon and Don went over the genealogy, and I became engrossed in a conversation with a fellow musician about our styles, repertoires. No hint of a notice of our contrasting skin color, no questions about how I fit into the picture.

We moved from group to group for an hour, speaking with Black families up from New York City, or upstate New York, others from Connecticut, Rhode Island. We seemed to be the only travelers down from Massachusetts. Donald voiced again and again his astonishment that no one was given a chance to speak for the Peters family, that very little recognition was given to the people who should have been central to the drama. Donald was convinced his destiny would have been totally different if Cesar and Lois had been sold down the coast to the Carolinas.

"I wouldn't be here today" echoed in his mind and in his talk, in our conversations.

The groups thinned, people headed outside and away to their destinations. Shortly, we found ourselves standing alone miles away, at the Peters house. Cesar and Lois actually did inherit the home from Master Peters, in spite of himself. We seemed to be the only ones who had made the trip from the film screening to this house, set well out of town in a farming district.

Rectangular, two-storied and solidly built, it stood staunchly on a small rise facing woods, with its back to the fields. The house had recently been saved from destruction, was quite empty and locked up tight, so we made our way around the outside, peering in windows, and imagining the events that might have occurred there, events that had influenced the Peters' life there. A fine colonial home, with large windows, it was not at all the 1700s saltbox home of the Jeffrey variety back in Charlestown, Rhode Island nor of the Deerfield style.

It looked relatively comfortable, echoing the pre-Revolutionary style of a country house belonging to an upper middle -class farmer. At one point we were joined in our solitary ambulation by a relatively scholarly gentleman, sporting an Irish wool walking hat and a pipe set at a jaunty angle. He too was a descendant of Cesar. He and Donald fell into a discussion regarding the various aspects of the Freemasons. He was of the Prince Hall Lodge, an exclusively black lodge, while Donald had joined the Grand Lodge of Massachusetts, the Blue Lodge.

Donald had broken the mold by not joining the black lodge of the other, and by insisting on joining his own local, heretofore all-white lodge.

Shannon and I continued our walk around the home, discovering an underground passage or possibly an escape route leading away from the cellar to the edge of the field. We spent time musing on the lives of those who had lived there, inspired by the capacity of old houses such as this to set loose the imagination of some spirits like us. We observed the house in silence, drawing forth the messages emanating from the ancient walls.

Presently, Donald and his new-found debating partner rounded a corner of the house, still talking lodges and and dueling over Freemason secrets. Donald was clearly not enjoying the tenor of the man's prodding. We helped change the subject, talking of Cesar's life in speculative terms.

Eventually we drifted to the car, pointed north to Massachusetts, and rode home. A few miles out of Hebron the talk resumed and Don clearly needed to get something off his chest.

"This was such a strange day. It started out with a real sense of excitement, and I'd say it ended with no small sense of disappointment. You know when I heard of the planned showing of a film that depicted my great, great, great, great grandfather Cesar Peters and his family's close brush with southern slavery, I was really excited about all this.

"That whole thing about no special seating for those of us descended from Cesar was one disappointment. I just was going to have to be satisfied to sit there and wait for this memorable moment in my life to unfold on the screen.

"To say I was disappointed would be an understatement. It was pretty evident that the film was not about my three times great grandfather Cesar, but it told the story of the man who struggled with his conscience about telling the truth or telling a lie. The truth would have sent the entire Peters family into slavery, and a lie would save them.

"A great story of morality, but not what I was led to expect. In telling the story on film, the Peters family didn't receive much attention. It seems to me that if a man had to struggle with his conscience about the fate of a black man, free or not, then it stands to reason that this black man must have been a worthy human being. It would have added to the movie that something of the nature of this family was depicted.

"During the drive to Hebron, I thought about what I might say should I get the chance to speak. It is not every day that you have the opportunity to come face to face with your past. If the lie had not been told, my family and I would not exist. I did not get the chance to speak but the feelings are still there, and just as strong."

At that point, Shannon, a bit exasperated, interrupted, saying:

" Dad, it just doesn't work that way, you would've been here one way or the other... you can't imagine that just one incident out of a whole ton of other events would've made for a different reality for us or our family..."

Don responded. "Look, I know I'm making this speech to just the two of you, the way I would've said it if I had the chance. But I'm convinced I wouldn't be here if not for Cesar, and if not for the man who struggled with his conscience and did the right thing."

He continued.

"You know, when we were standing in front of Rev. Peters' house, where Cesar was a slave, I was given a stark lesson in the difficult life lived by slaves in contrast to their white masters. The house occupied by Rev. Peters was of a fine colonial style of the time. In the back portion of the house is the ramshackle quarters where the slaves, where WE lived. Those quarters were built of mismatched scrap boards where the wind could get through, and the cold New England winters must have been unbearable.

"I'd say 'Thank you!' to the descendants of the man who struggled with his conscience and perhaps told a lie to save Cesar.

"And to my great great great great grandfather I'd say 'Thank you Cesar, for being worthy!'

Donald looked at me with an uncharacteristically stern look.

"That's what I would have said to all of them if I had the chance.

Did you get it all down? Because that's what I want in the book."

I did get it all down. And it is in the book.

Chapter 13

Trip to Narragansett 2010

"You will remember this," said Awasoos. *"Time can flow forward and can flow back. If you have truly been given the Sight, you can walk in-between"*

There was one more journey we knew we had to make. Joseph Jeffrey had not only been at the beginning of our 300-year odyssey to the present, to this place. He had also done another important thing that helped link us to him. He had built a house next to his sawmill on Narragansett lands that in fact has been preserved as a bridge between tribal culture and English colonial culture. He had built it in the colonial style, moving from the *wetu* of the tribal seasonal life to a home built of wood, nails, mortar and bricks on a permanent foundation. A house that would not move. This house is now listed on the National Registry of Historic Places, and as such is protected, preserved, and still standing! This house was to be our ultimate destination, this would bring our journey full circle; we would stand where Joseph had stood, we would touch the wood that he had cut, the walls that he had built. We would find his spirit there.

Easier said than done. Barbara got on the trail. A call to the Narragansett Tribal Headquarters got her nowhere. They did not know who Joseph Jeffrey was, nor did they have any idea where his house might be. They suggested we call the Chamber of Commerce, or the Town Hall. No one there had heard of the Jeffrey House either, even though it was on the Registry of Historic Places. Eventually Barbara tracked down the State Archeologist who of course could find the records of the house and the file of research that led to its historical designation.

Once the file was located, it was a question of organizing the trip to seek out the house. I called the current owner, Anne Marshall, who volunteered to meet us whenever we decided to make the trip. We were eager to go sooner than later, and the opportunity presented itself when we discovered that the annual Narragansett Gathering in Charlestown, Rhode Island, takes place on the second weekend in August. This gathering at the corn harvest had been occurring at this place and time for the past 334 recorded years, and for a hundred generations before that. We had to be there for the Gathering. Things were converging fast.

The night before the first trip to the Jeffrey house found me wide awake with anxious excitement. I had gone to the cemetery at Laurel Hill in Deerfield to tell Betsy I was going back, and telling her I really didn't know what to expect.

I was bringing Deerfield corn with me, bought at the Ciesluk roadside stand at the foot of the hill below the cemetery. I left one ear of corn on the gravesite as an offering to my ancestors Betsy and Sarah, and their family. The rest I would take down to Rhode Island to offer to the Narragansett Medicine Woman about whom I had heard much. I kept one ear of corn for the Jeffrey House when we found it.

In the twilight, this night before the trip, I sat quietly in the lilac bower Judah had planted, as I looked over his house in the dusk.

I've always pictured this house and its peak like the prow of a ship, running north and south. It seems to always have sailed on, since 1872, through hurricanes and blizzards, sheltering humble generations of my family since Judah got it. He had lived out his life and died in it, and now it had come down to me, when I came back to dwell here with my own family. This is the first permanent house the family has had since leaving Joseph's house ten generations ago. The Indian house in Narragansett of 1720 to this house in 1872: Rhode Island to Lyme to Windsor to Deerfield to Millers Falls.

Tomorrow will I come face-to-face with my 7th great grandfather? Or just his house? Will I sleep at all tonight?

The descendants of Joseph began a long journey from the reservation to Lyme, then up the river, generation after generation to Deerfield. All these years. And now me here, standing on their shoulders. It was the night before my departure, and I was finally ready to set out on the journey to find the place where it all started.

The following morning we headed out early, in two cars. Donald and I drove together alone, the rest of the family followed us respecting our wishes to complete this journey together. We needed to be just the two of us, children of the same great grandmother. Our lives had been radically different, mine white, his black, lived out a few miles from each other, never knowing the other existed. But each of us was possessed by a drive, a yearning to know where we came from. Each of us had reached positions of modest influence, of leadership in our two worlds. Now we knew where an important part of our story began, we were going back to a house, a homestead, to something of a destiny towards which we had been journeying for a lifetime.

We left at the break of day, and traveled on in silence. The warm August morning hung low on the fields of corn and tobacco along our route, fog nestled here and there over water and low ground, already dissipating in the rays of the sun angling obliquely across the landscape. Not needing to speak, each of us remained deep in our own thoughts. I was retracing the route, the steps covered generations ago, new to me, new to my eyes, although I had gone up and down this part of the road before. South we went, following the slow-moving Connecticut River until Hartford when we angled off towards the southeast. We would not see Windsor, Wallingford, Lyme, or East Haddam today. These were names that were a constant in the early days of our family, town names that resonated in my mind as though they were exotic places lost in time. We were headed straight as an arrow, or at least as straight as Routes 291, 15, and 2 permitted.

After Hartford, we began speaking, as the scenery changed from the lush valley of our homeland to the rolling wooded hills and low woodlands of mid-Connecticut. We went over again the lineage, the connections, family stories, almost reciting to each other. This I suppose is how oral history continues, people tell each other, and tell the younger ones, all about the story of the family.

We talked again of Betsy, Charles, Judah and Sarah, and all those various men named Solomon in the family. We talked about what else we needed to explore, what mysteries remained, what graves were left to find, what tribal links between Narragansett, Nehantic, Pequot, and Mohegan remained to be investigated. We went over and over the aftermath of the Pequot War as though it happened last year, we talked of the King Phillip's War that raged throughout our homelands pitting Pocumtuck, Sokoki, Nipmuk, Narragansett and Wampanoag against the English intruders.

Before long we were passing the turquoise blue towers of the Pequot FoxWoods complex, garish and rich and out of place.

We soon found ourselves in the state of Rhode Island, motoring through scrub oaks and pitch pines, on the way to the reservation and the Gathering.

Our intention was to get to the Narragansett Church in time for the service at 11. As we approached the gathering site along a winding dirt road through pitch pines, distant drumming began reaching our ears, much like a distant heartbeat. Presently we came to a table set up on the side of the road, where several elders sat while two younger tribal members collected the entry fee. One of the elders was Dr. Ella Sekatau, Tribal Medicine Woman, historian and tribal genealogist. I approached her and offered her the corn from Pocumtuck for her family.

We parked and waited for the other car in our excursion to catch up with us. We stepped from our capsule of time and stories, out into the warm sun, under the pines, and into another world yet again. Native people had arrived in their campers and were sitting smoking in lawn chairs around campfires, others were busying themselves preparing outfits and regalia for the dancing. Drums resonated throughout the woods, louder now.

We made our way to the gathering place. The church was set off to the right of the circle where the dances and ceremonies were to be. The church doors were open, hymns floated out to reach our ears. A gracious woman greeted us, handed each of us a hymnal, and we moved to the rows of pews that faced the door. This was different, I thought. Usually the pews face the pulpit near the altar and the parishioners have their backs to the door. Why were they facing the door and the windows? Off to the side, a woodstove and its piping occupied a corner and reached up to the high ceiling.

The singing over, Alberta Wilcox of the Church Board greeted us all, welcoming us to the church and its annual Gathering, now in its 334th recorded year. Oral history relates that this August Meeting has occurred on the 6th Moon since time immemorial. I knew that the continuity of the annual Corn Harvest Gathering had played an important part in establishing, according to the Federal government's criteria, federal recognition of the Narragansett Tribe. Mrs. Wilcox explained the history of the church and the unusual placement of the pews.

"We had to be able to see who was coming down the path" she said. "We needed to know who was approaching, who was going to come in the door, friend or foe."

As the service drew to a close, the deaconess asked us to stand, to grasp the hand of the person to our right and left, to form a ring, a circle. She then asked if anyone would like to say anything to the group before parting. My blood began thundering in my ears, I knew I would have to say what was on my heart. This was my unique chance. One after the other, individuals asked that loved ones be remembered, that we think of those who were no longer living, of those who were struggling with disease, of those who had gone to Iraq or Afghanistan. Others asked that President Obama be given strength to succeed in bringing the country together.

I knew that the time had come to speak, it had all come down to this specific moment, now that we were so close to our beginnings. I held Donald's hand on one side of me, an unknown woman's on the other side. The circle extended thusly around the room. I summoned up my inner, louder voice so that I could be heard without faltering with emotion, and I said something like:

"I'd like to give thanks for the guidance I've received on this journey. Over the past year, I have found again members of my family that were lost to memory. I've found my cousin Donald, and we have traveled here together as cousins and brothers to this church of our ancestors. I'm thankful to have met him, and that we are here again in this church. Our ancestor Joseph Jeffrey was a member of this church almost

300 years ago, and now we have come back here to renew our connection to this place."

I tried to calm my heart, to keep my voice from cracking, to control the emotion welling up in my eyes.

Then Donald spoke, his firm practiced baritone continued my thoughts when I had stopped speaking.

"We've come back to this church. I'm thankful for the spirit that has led us here. I have to say, I've been to other tribal gatherings and powwows, but this is the place where I feel most at home, most welcome."

As other voices added their thanks and wishes, the woman to the left of me whose hand I held said something to the group which sounded strangely familiar:

"I'm happy to be back here in this church where my 7th great grandfather once stood, when he was once a member of this congregation."

Wait a minute, I thought.

Our 7th great grandfather Joseph was also a member of this congregation! So the three of us standing there had connections to the same generation of 300 years ago?

We needed to find out who this person was.

Outside in the bright sun, after the service was over, we made our way to her, where she was standing with her husband.

"Hello! I couldn't help but be startled by what you said in there. So your 7th great grandfather was a member of this church? So was mine. At the same time."

She replied:

"Well, my ancestor was Toby Coyess. He was part of the Anti-Sachem Party and they were trying to get rid of Tom Ninigret. Tom was getting into debt all the time and selling tribal lands. Toby eventually got to be the oldest member of the Tribe, and lived many years after Tom Ninigret died."

I remembered Toby's name from the Joseph Fish Diaries of 1765-1776. I had the sinking feeling that this Toby was somehow partly responsible for Joseph Jeffrey losing his home, under pressure from the Anti-Sachem Party and Tom Ninigret's creditors. I related the story to her. She didn't know Joseph's name, but I told her of the sawmill, and of the Jeffrey house still standing. I told her of the exile and slow wandering of Joseph's family and descendants back to Black Point in East Lyme and then up the Connecticut River Valley.

"So in a way, your ancestor was responsible for our ancestor losing his home! That set off an unbelievable chain of events that placed Donald and me in the Connecticut River Valley, and then brought us back here!" I said this in mock anger. She laughed, not knowing what to think.

I was about to take her hand in a gesture of peace-making. Which I did.

I was about to say that our chance meeting was an indication of the spirits of reconciliation.

But I didn't.

I held back. Could I speak for Joseph Jeffrey who had fought for so many years to get his house back? To get back the house that he had built with his own hands with lumber he had cut and hewn in his own sawmill? It had been taken from him in 1769 when he was an old man, by the members of this Anti-Sachem Party. Was it within my power, within my rights, within the rights of Donald and myself as Joseph's representatives to forgive?

I had a pretty good sense that Joseph's spirit was not yet at rest, even after 300 years. Something told me he needed something else. He and his children had fought too hard to get his house and land back. His right to be there was granted at the outset, before Tom Ninigret, back to Tom's ancestor Charles Ninigret, the great Ninigret II, back when the reservation was founded in 1709. Joseph had been a powerful member of Ninigret's inner circle, a member of the Sachem's council, and in his eyes, he had earned the right to the house he had built. So I held my tongue.

I could not yet forgive, nor was it in my power. I could not forgive the descendant of a man who had caused my ancestors to leave this homeland, and to wander for generations. We smiled and posed for a photograph. But we needed to hear from Joseph before Donald and I could forgive. It was not yet within our power. Luckily just then, the Grand Entry of the Indian nations was forming and we moved away to watch hundreds of members from the assembled tribes make their way chanting and dancing into the sacred circle.

By early afternoon, we felt we had to leave the Gathering and finish our pilgrimage.

We left the grounds and wove our way through the reservation lands back to the main road, the drumbeats still following us. We were to meet Anne Marshall, who now owned the Joseph Jeffrey house and who was eager to meet the descendants of the man who had built it. We followed the winding road through neighborhoods that looked quite middle-class, with middle-class white people mowing lawns, cooking on outdoor grills, much like any woodland neighborhood in any semi-rural development . I had expected something else.

When we reached the sawmill site, Anne was waiting for us in the driveway. We were quickly to learn that she is an extremely gracious woman, fond of researching this house that she had owned since the 1960s, and she was deeply conscious of the momentous occasion this was in our lives.

The house stands on a small rise, looking very much like the houses in Old Deerfield, shingled, clapboarded and weathered. I walked around it slowly as if in a daze, trying to stay in touch with what I was feeling. Was I feeling anything? Maybe I was trying too hard.

Before coming here, I had studied the architect's Statement of Significance that had propelled this house onto the National Registry of Historic Places. I knew by heart that the foundations were made of fieldstone, that this house was a "one and a half story gambrel roof center chimney frame dwelling". It had been written that this house was of a standard 18th century five-room plan with an off-center chimney. I knew that the staircase led to three upper chambers, and that the peak section of the gambrel roof rafters are marked in Roman numerals I-VIII. I had read the report many times and knew all the specifics of its architecture, or at least what I could understand.

The statement also said that the house and sawmill were built on lands controlled by the Narragansetts, and that Joseph "had demonstrated an early, conscious and proficient use of early American colonial building norms." In fact, Joseph's house was a rare example of early Indian adaptation of colonial styles. Joseph was somewhat of an innovator, and his work was significant enough to be preserved and protected as part of the national historic heritage.

So I knew, we knew, his spirit was here in the wood, in the rooms, somewhere. But where? I was conscious that we were merely visitors, even tourists, traipsing through the rooms, talkative, excited, noisy, snapping photographs. No way was Joseph going to show himself.

I was drawn to the central room around the chimney. It was dark, low-ceilinged. The small colonial windows let in little light. The wainscoting was dark, aged, cured with centuries of wood smoke. It was formed of broad colonial-style boards yet I found familiarity in its function and appearance. I had replaced old wainscoting in my own house, Judah's house, years before, instinctively, unknowingly repeating the work and actions of traditional builders.

This room would be the room to which I would journey back. Near the fireplace and in the low-ceilinged room is where I would find Joseph. Maybe not today, maybe only in a dream. But this room was where he was, the wainscoting and fireplace showed that to me, it was here, and I had to be patient.

With that sense, I stepped back out into the bright day, to finish the circling of the entire house, visiting with the resident cats, and arriving at the mill pond. Our guide Anne, a retired school teacher herself, was clearly tuned in to the significance of the place, the significance of the fact that Joseph's blood descendants were standing with her on the overgrown mill dam. We stood and looked on the tranquil pond.

"Another man, also a descendant of Joseph Jeffrey was here last year. I can get you his address. His name is Eric Smith"

Donald and I looked at each other. Could this Smith tie in with the mysterious Smith who was the father whom Judah had never met? Another new trail to pursue.

(We were later to learn how we were connected to Eric. He is a descendant of our Joseph Jeffrey, and Joseph's great-grandson Asa Jeffrey. Asa was our own Rebecca Jeffrey's brother. Rebecca herself had remained in the Connecticut River Valley and her line led directly to Donald and me generations later, up the Connecticut River Valley. Asa Jeffrey had gone to Brothertown in upstate New York with Samson Occum as had many New England Indians, where they settled there as guests of the Iroquois nation.)

We lingered by the pond, telling stories, exchanging bits of information we had culled concerning the Ninigret family, Canonchet, the complicated internal tribal politics of the Narragansetts, and anything else we knew of Joseph.

The sun was slanting from the west through the pitch pines and pin oaks. It was time to start back to the valley. We said our goodbyes and rode back in silence. We mulled over our individual thoughts until the first stop for coffee. That loosened our tongues and thoughts, and there was no stop to the talking, the connecting of random thoughts culled from this momentous day, as we began blending impressions and events of this day into a new chapter of our mutual family oral history.

Chapter 14

The Circle Now Unbroken

In the parlor, in Judah's house, in my house now, we sit in silence. It has been a long afternoon and evening of story-telling and remembrance. Many ancestors have come to tell us their stories, completing the cycle begun so long ago in the Jeffrey house.

It's time for Donald and me to speak, to bring this story of the family full circle. He and I have now traveled many a mile together on the trail of our ancestors, through both time, and space. We've been back to our roots in Narragansett country, to the Peters house in Hebron, and to the Nehantic lands in Lyme. We've seen Deerfield now with different eyes, journeyed to the graves of Betsy Strong, Sarah and William Barnes, to those of Judah and Lizzie. We've spent countless hours reconstructing the lives of our mutual ancestors. We have relearned the connection between Betsy and her children Judah, Sarah, Solomon, and Charles, a connection that had been lost to family memory, clearly on purpose.

We had lived in different worlds separated by a few miles. The revelations of the past five years have been astounding: our families have been reconnected, we've learned more about our origins, we have been guided by our ancestors.

Donald rises and steps forward to the center of the semi-circle where we are all seated, all of us from the two worlds. He carries his eighty years well. He is now the patriarch, descended from one of Betsy's sons, Charles Scott, Judah's brother. He projects dignity and a tranquil spirit. He seems to look somewhere beyond, into the distance, into the past. His hat is carefully placed on the wicker chair next to him.

His voice, and his choice of words, are clear and articulate.

"I was born in 1929. That date seems and sounds like so long ago. My father was Solomon Scott and my mother Bernice Clark Scott. I have six brothers and a sister: Jerry, Melvin (Rudolph), Shirley, Stanley, Ted, Billy (Solomon) and Gary. I spent most of my early years in Greenfield, where it seems like there had always been a small community of colored families: Harris, Scott, Peters, Barnes, McCain, O'Hare, O'Neill, and Stone.

We all pretty much lived near one another in the same working class neighborhoods. In those days, quite a few minority families lived in the area of Deerfield Street. That neighborhood was like a Little America because there were so many ethnic groups: Poles, Lithuanians, Italians, French Canadians, lots of colored families. Below Bank Row, that whole section of town was working class.

I can now see what probably brought us to the neighborhood around Deerfield Street. My great grandmother Betsy Strong and her brother Solomon had moved there in the 1870s when Cheapside and Deerfield Street were a part of Deerfield and not Greenfield. It became the part of town that people of our social class started out, before moving uptown.

The family oral history passed down to us was that we were a little different, in that we had Indian blood, probably Pequot. Of course, with all the research we've done recently, I can see we are more likely a blend of Pequot, Mohegan, Nehantic, and Narragansett.

Those tribes all lived so close to one another, there was quite a lot of mixing, and their history so turbulent. My uncle

Walter used to talk about that connection. He had a lot of stories about our people going back generations, a lot of oral history. I wish I had written down what he told us, I wish I had asked more questions.

We all got by as best we could. The Depression and the War made life hard for everybody, but we looked out for one another, and we made it through.

My father Sol was a guiding force in the family. He was a hard working man all those years, and often held down two jobs. He had done all kinds of things to make sure we had meals and a roof over our heads, which wasn't always easy. He had wanted to be an electrician, but no white electrician would take him on as an apprentice. As I said, there were only a few colored families in town, but just the same there was no small amount of prejudice. We were accepted in the schools and in the workplace, but as we grew older, we learned what the limits were to our interactions with the rest of the town.

Sol taught us by example not to pay attention to the color of people. He was the one in the neighborhood who all the kids, colored or not, came to for help, from removing a loose tooth to fixing bikes. They all said "Go see Mr. Scott, he'll take care of it." Just the same, he always felt he had faced discrimination in the school, he always resented that the coach kept him off the track team because although he was the fastest youngster in the school, it wouldn't do to have a black as the star of the track team. That would have been around 1922.

My father had been a truck driver, a janitor, a boiler room worker. That job cost him a lung. There wasn't much equipment in those days to protect workers' eyes, or ears, to protect them from the dust. He wound up with a collapsed lung. Later he went to work at the Tap and Die like a lot of the men in my family.

Sol was really a role model for me and my siblings. He was a strong, no nonsense father blessed with a fundamental good nature. He had an inner strength, and although he didn't have a lot of education, he had a natural curiosity, he was a great reader, and taught himself many things. He had a manner about him. He had a quite noble bearing, he was an impeccable dresser. He had a lot of self-discipline, and he had strong common sense. Sol wasn't much of a talker, very stoic really. But he did like talking about the outdoors, and about fishing.

My mother, on the other hand, was the one we could talk to. She taught us how to take care of the house and help her. She encouraged me to sing. She sang at church and gave me my love of music. We were always in church with her. She even wanted me to become a minister at one point, after I gave a sermon one Sunday! She was a contralto, and when I said I couldn't reach her high notes (since I was a baritone), she said "Yes you can!" She made me try. I always remember that.

In school, I was always interested in history, and that has always sustained me during my life. Maybe I got my love of reading and history from Sol who was a great reader, as I mentioned. That's some of what I have from my parents, a love of history, reading, music, and I learned from them how to stick to a job, to keep improving on what I had. That has been very important, all during my life.

I've learned so much about the family recently that just wasn't known or knowable to us before. If only I had taken down all the stories from my Uncle Walter. He was the one who, like in most families, carried on the stories of our family. I wish we had listened a little closer to him and to his stories, a lot of that is lost now.

This search we've been on for the past five years now is probably a second chance for me, to recover much that we thought had been lost. We do have a history, there are many in our lineage who make us proud, upon whose shoulders we have climbed to get where we are.

That day back in the Narragansett Church was one of those rare moments in life when things get crystal-clear, when you sense a welcoming spirit, when you feel truly *at home*. We were among *our* people, we were in the church of *our* family, reconnecting over 300 years. Later on, that same day, when we visited Joseph Jeffrey's house, the same feeling washed over me. How many people get to stand in their ancestor's home? How many can sense the presence of an ancestor while standing where he stood, in the house that he built? I *came* from here. I have a history, and the people who lived in those rooms set that history in motion way back then.

As for my own personal story, it seems like I've always gone against the grain a bit. Maybe I got that from the Jeffreys who, way back, stayed involved in civil rights , just wouldn't let things be, kept pushing the margins. I didn't necessarily have anything to prove, but I just followed my natural inclination to keep moving upwards. I've always had a sense of service, that mold was set back in high school, even before, looks like I was just born that way.

A big part of my life became my work with the Masons. It wasn't easy for a person like me to get into the Lodge I'm now in, since most men of color joined the Prince Hall Lodge down in Springfield. But I wanted to be in the Lodge in my own town, so I kept at it. I've moved up through the ranks ever since. I became a Thirty-Third Degree Scottish Rite Mason, and I've now reached the level of Grand Lecturer.

That probably sums up the course of my life: service to others, the Church, family, music, my love of history. I worked at fulfilling what I was meant to be and to do. Where did I get the impulse to do all that? Was it from Joseph Jeffrey, and all his descendants who were activists and leaders? Was it from

Rudolph Scott or Charles Scott? From Cesar and Lois, from Sol, or Bernice?

Probably came from all of them, that whole line. We stand on the shoulders of those who came before, those who put us here. Now it seems I know better who I am, by knowing more about where I come from.

And knowing that, now after this journey, I walk a little taller"

Donald has spoken, and now it comes down to me. It has been a long and winding path, full of twists and turns of fate and destiny, that returned me here to live among family, even to find them, to discover those who go all the way back to Joseph. My own personal story is woven all through the pages I've written here. As with all of you, there are many dimensions to my life's story. Yet parts of it, the coincidences, the chance meetings that have brought me here to this room before you, those parts have become the most important to me.

"In sifting through my story, what first brought me back here more than forty years ago, was this house, and my grandfather Abe, Judah's son. There was a point in my existence when I lived far from here, but somehow I sensed the moment had arrived to come back to this green valley home. I had crossed oceans, been high up in the snow-covered Alps, visited deserts, lived alone in a mountain village in North Africa.

When I knew it was time to return, my small family and I had actually been living in Paris for several years. When, in that wonderful city, I found myself scrutinizing the Eiffel Tower for a glimpse of the fierce little falcon who lived in the steel girders far from the wilds of field and woods, or when I lingered long in the Impressionist museum, lost in the

146

snowscapes of Monet, Pissarro and Sisley, longing for the country, for the familiar beauty of snow-filled woods, the graceful slope of white-blanketed fields, well, then I knew it was time to come home to my Connecticut River Valley.

Amidst those pangs of longing for this valley I received word that Abe was failing.

Like the rest of his grandchildren, I was strongly drawn to Abe, my maternal grandfather. There was a connivance between Abe and his grandchildren, and I was part of that. I used to come to stay in this house whenever I could, and living only four miles away, it wasn't hard to get here, especially once I got a bicycle.

Coming here then, it felt like I was falling into a time warp. I had early on developed a love of old things. Time did seem to have stopped here at some time in the 1940s. Even now I can picture my mother, her brothers and sisters in this parlor, or outside, a photograph in black and white, standing in the un-mown grass in the back yard of those days, with clotheslines, chicken coops, and lilacs in the background.

This house stands on the edge of a dark woodland, the street and sidewalk end here, and beyond lie trees and creatures living thereabouts that time seems to have forgotten.

These woods seemed wilder to me at the time, wilder than near my parents' home. Different, ancient birds sang in the twilight here, the river was more sparkling, rushing over rounded stones, different from the wide and deep slow-moving Connecticut.

The fact that I was born on the shores of the Connecticut, where my early life was spent, not five miles from where we are now, has made all the difference to my story.

I came into this world on Christmas Eve in 1946, just after the War when my father Arthur had come home from the

Pacific in late 1945. He made it back safe and sound, not even scratched after four years on various aircraft carriers, and after flying hundreds of bombing runs, torpedo runs. He married into the Smith family, into Judah's family. He married one of Abe's daughters, a slip of a girl named Shirley, my mother, and they began a family in our little home above the Narrows on the Connecticut River. The new place was close enough to her home so that she could walk back to her mother's house if she felt homesick, and she often did. I've only recently realized and put into words the effect of living on these rivers would have on my life.

My sister Susan and I lived in relative peace and sibling competition. We shared a love of nature and history. We were blessed with the warmth, comfort, and nurturing provided by our hard-working father, and vigilant, loving mother.

But it's Abe and this house that are entwined inextricably with my life and this story.

I know now how much of a role this homestead was actually going to play, thirty years after I moved back here, when we began prying open the secrets of this house and its memories of generations past.

Abe himself was born here, in this room, which was smaller then, when it was used for birthing, nursing the sick, and dying. He was almost born under the big maple tree still standing down the pasture path a little way from here. That 1st of May, Lizzie was in the pasture near the Millers River working with the others, and felt her time was coming on, as Pete tells it. And after having brought six children already into this world, this last child came forth with no problem. That would've been in 1896.

Abe was always the apple of Lizzie's eye. He always played the cunning rascal, a great teller of tall tales, one of those liars who would squint at you to see if you believed him, to see if he had taken you in. He kept all of us in stitches with his old-fashioned jokes, his feigned gruffness.

Yet he never talked about his father's family. I knew almost nothing of his own youth, of what his parents were like, and he never really spoke seriously about the old people. He spoke only of Judah as JW, or the Old Gent. Maybe, looking back, that was part of the conspiracy of silence. Now I know of course that he knew plenty, but he never told us anything back then.

There was something in his feigned roughness, his untamed nature and an air he had about himself of being stuck in that time warp, that fascinated me. Even into the 1970s he was never without his wool cap, summer or winter, a corn cob pipe jammed into the corner of his mouth, his workman's blue chambray shirt reflecting the startling pale China blue of his eyes. Those eyes often caught you in their foxy squint, checking to see if you were paying attention to his tricks and little lies.

I can still remember some elderly ladies, slightly rouged up and all bright lipstick, remarking to me one time in a friend's parlor: "Oh, so you're *Abe Smith's* grandson?"

I can still picture the knowing twinkle in their eyes and sly winks. I sure would like to know what that was about!

So you see, when I heard he was failing, back from Paris we came, back to this house, naively thinking that we could take care of him, naively thinking that he would let us! Pete had warned us that it was more than we could handle, "taking care of an old man like that."

In fact it was never to be that way. I had always imagined that he would die like one of the old oaks on the high edge of the pasture. I thought that he'd come crashing down, ripping branches, thrashing through the younger trees, thundering to the ground, causing the smaller maple saplings to snap and spring back, swaying in the new space he left with his falling.

It wasn't like that. He had to go quietly in his sleep, silently, like most of us would want.

We didn't respect his wishes after his death:

he wanted to be buried standing up, with his favorite fly-fishing pole in his hand, Polish kielbasa sausage and a bottle of beer in his wicker creel. Don't know where he got that oft-repeated desire he made us promise to fulfill. That's just how it was with him, you couldn't really tell what he was up to.

I needed to tell you about him, because he should not be forgotten and he played an important role in this story. He was the other link to the family's past, just as sure as was Pete, in helping us reconnect. Without him, we would not be in this house, and the walls would not be able to tell us what they remember. So, because of Abe, my little family and I settled back here, and when things finally began falling into place, this house has played its role.

For when you live in an old house, especially the one that five generations of your own kin have lived in, your sense of your own house and land becomes part of your being, your generational memory is renewed so naturally that you feel the depth of the connection with it, without consciously seeking it.

In an ancestral landscape, there is a familiarity with every tree, every hidden corner in the woods, every spring that flows upward to the surface to fill the woodland ponds with icy water. Each stone and tree has a soul. Each creature is familiar, an extension of its own past generations that dwelled on the edges of my own ancestors' existence. They recognize my form moving through the woods, my scent is familiar, they know who I am.

There are places, perhaps for each of us, where our physical world and the spirit world are more close to one another than anywhere else. These are the places where the boundary of those two worlds disappears, where it is easy to pass between.

That is what this house does. It's a sort of passageway between the two worlds. Here, great-grandfather and family gathered, lived and raised their children and their children's children. They all walked through that very door which has not been changed or replaced, out of the love and respect for old things. Their hands turned that doorknob countless times, they and their kin, my kin, our kin, stepped over that very threshold. The steps of Judah, Lizzie, Betsy, Sarah, Solomon and Charles all trod these very boards of this floor beneath us. Their eyes gazed out of the same rippled window glass still here in this parlor, and these very walls have now welcomed them back again, old arguments dissolved, old shames banished.

So I came back to this family house, not knowing all of this at the time, just as surely as I was brought back by some unknown hand, and we made a life for ourselves here. This house provided the connection and the key that led to the opening up of all these mysteries and secrets, all these restless spirits.

We came back here, opened windows to air and light. We came back here and stayed, and now slowly but surely the real reason that drew us here has revealed itself to us.

It could easily have been otherwise. But like many aspects of life, it was meant to happen. Our family story pieced itself together when it was the right time, when the right people appeared, when Pete told me her secret, when Barbara came back to her home town, when Donald answered the phone. When we were ready.

Those of you from the two worlds who are here have told your stories, have renewed the circle of family. We have learned to praise and respect those who have placed us here, we know better who we are, and we know why we're here.

Betsy H. Strong – Donald B. Scott

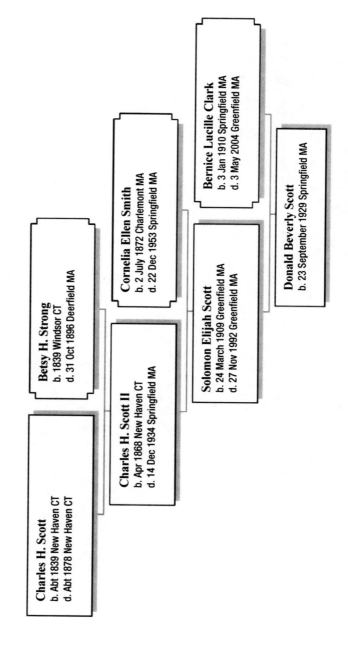

Charles H. Scott
b. Abt 1839 New Haven CT
d. Abt 1878 New Haven CT

Betsy H. Strong
b. 1839 Windsor CT
d. 31 Oct 1896 Deerfield MA

Charles H. Scott II
b. Apr 1868 New Haven CT
d. 14 Dec 1934 Springfield MA

Cornelia Ellen Smith
b. 2 July 1872 Charlemont MA
d. 22 Dec 1953 Springfield MA

Solomon Elijah Scott
b. 24 March 1909 Greenfield MA
d. 27 Nov 1992 Greenfield MA

Bernice Lucille Clark
b. 3 Jan 1910 Springfield MA
d. 3 May 2004 Greenfield MA

Donald Beverly Scott
b. 23 September 1929 Springfield MA

Chapter 15

The Grandson Wishes To Remember

"What the son wishes to forget, the grandson wishes to remember".
---Third Generation Searchers

This is a phrase that I came across in one of the many readings over the years. It's a familiar phrase to those of us who are of the third generation, and who are looking for our ancestors. I found it had resonance with me, and so I'm using it here. It is not original with me but it is an image that is powerful.

This story has become a long journey of learning and remembering. It would seem that there is always one in each generation who has the responsibility to do this, to be a keeper of the stories, to carry the light of family knowledge. Most of us who choose that role don't know why, but we do know that we have the responsibility for that task. Perhaps we may feel something that others can't feel, a different pain, a different sadness, a different longing; the burden and the need to look further and deeper than the others may shape our life. There occur circumstances, chance meetings, a certain sudden frame of mind that erases the passage of time that are signs to us. For me it was the murmurings of the river, the fleeting shadows of spirits in the woods. These signs show us that we are the ones given the responsibility to learn, remember, and pass on the knowledge.

This story that began with a simple remark and a photograph turned into a journey to answer questions about self identity and lost connections to family, to explain why we look the way we do, to explain how we got here, to explain the strange visions that come up unexpectedly from deep within. This story turned into a very personal one of a family with mixed ethnicity, of American Indians, Africans and Whites from southern New England, a family that collectively felt the need to hide the mixture of bloods. It was no longer a simple recounting of the lives of those who came before, but even more it became an attempt to imagine what complex forces were exerted on the generations before us.

I've learned the story of the multiple descendants of a number of informal, interracial marriages. I've tried to understand and relate how this family of mine tried to deal with the complexities of our own miscegenous, exogamous marriages that actually were not uncommon at one point in our nation's history.

This family of mine chose to live under the denial of their real origins and of the real blend of races in our blood. They suffered the real fears of discrimination, and of being exposed as less than white. The story became a personal recounting of ethnicity, class, race, denial, assimilation, a loss and retrieval of self identity.

I am fortunate in that this story has a certain uniqueness and coherence, yet it could resonate with many because of so many of us have hidden family secrets. It was also helpful that this history evolved in a relatively confined geographic space over three hundred years, and within ten generations of family in southern New England.

Besides the above, the task was somewhat facilitated by the fact that considerable research had already been done by specialists and experts on certain members of our extended family. The records reveal much about the personal lives, the contemporaries, fortunes, and destinies of specific ancestors.

Yet this narrative is intended as a personal story, not a history text. Through the synthesis of all this research, family lore and oral histories, I've sought to look at my own origins, my own multiple identities, the forces that make me who I am, standing here at the beginning of the 21st century.

I can be sure now: the one in each generation who steps forward and chooses to remember, to claim it all, to gain a greater self understanding for those who will follow, that is certainly me. I know who I am now, and I know what I was meant to do.

In these pages, I have consulted with the ancestors, and spoken for them. I was given a task, and I have had to do it right. I know that those who came before gave me this story, helped me put it into words, and in fact, the story has written itself.

What we've learned and revealed, the conclusions we've reached are open to criticism. These days, now in the early part of the 21st century, it may seem that some of the stigma from the 19th and 20th centuries has eased. At the very least we can observe that mixed marriages, the mixing of bloods and races has become more commonplace. We can hope that the children of these marriages may no longer face the same major obstacles to advancement, to success, that Judah's siblings and their children did, in this still very white-dominated American society. It would seem that skill, intelligence, character, and ambition actually may one day trump skin color, in spite of the daily reminders that ignorance and racial hatred still persist.

In my own way, I lay claim to the right to know about my own identity in its entirety, to claim it not only for myself, but for my brothers and sisters, my whole extended family, as we plunge headlong into the new century.

I have said here what we have learned, about where I come from, as a part of a story, a history. It has been my good fortune to be able to participate in the sharing of this small story, another tale entwined in the varied strands of human existence. May you receive it in the spirit in which it is offered.

What I have learned has come to me from many different sources and many voices. I've just sought to blend them here, to recount what they have meant to us, without claiming any of this as original, new knowledge. It became new knowledge for us, so I have used this knowledge obtained from others, in explaining how I came to learn, and to remember what was hidden and denied for three generations of my own family.

Part of this narrative has become an effort to retrieve the threads of my mixed race immediate family, most members of which were assimilated into white society and who consequently disappeared, at least as People of Color, back in the 1900s. So a part of this effort involved writing about what it is like to be a grandchild of a mixed Indian/White/Black family in whom the tribal affiliation disappeared three generations ago. The African American identity was denied and hidden starting two generations ago, and now what is left is what was then the only accepted and acceptable affiliation, that of the dominant group, that of white society. So as a descendant of a number of prominent Tribal and African American New England families, and likely a fairly prominent White Yankee family, it has become a focal point of my life to retrace and record (with plenty of help), the collective experiences of the more than ten generations of extended family that put us here.

Now, if I'm the grandson who wishes to remember for all of the family at this point, I also have to take stock of what I have learned, what clues have come my way, to help understand the grandfathers and their fathers, the grandmothers and their mothers.

Central to what we have learned in this search to recover what was lost or hidden is the story of Betsy Strong's three informal, exogamous marriages, and the destinies of her four children who came from those marriages. Each of those mixed race children chose, or were led to choose group affiliations based on skin color.

The one of course that I'm the most familiar with is Judah. Because of his light skin, he passed for white by 1880, although his ties to his mother's tribal people, and to his siblings of color, were part of his existence, part of his identity. These ties were shown to be part of his marriage and household until a certain point in his life, when in the social dynamic of this country, mixed race (especially for those with *any* black blood) became a strong impediment to social advancement, to the ability of his children to get ahead. The case in point which illustrates this best in my family's history was that in which his son Douglass had his future and promise of success in the sports world curtailed in 1912 because of allegations that he had "black blood", which indeed he had, a fact that succeeding generations of the family felt they needed to bury and deny.

It became an imperative in my family to choose an exclusive affiliation with white society. Lizzie Moir enabled this, as a white Scottish Protestant who forged the way for her children and grandchildren to join the dominant group. Seen from our current vantage point, the generations from Judah and Lizzie to those of us who are their great-grandchildren (a period roughly from 1900-2007), bracket the duration of the denial of our origins. It would seem that there was be a beginning, and therefore should be an ending, to that stigma and denial.

What should have been an asset in cultural terms, in terms of the richness of ethnic references of dual identities, became a serious obstacle to assimilation into white society, the only society in which one could get ahead at the time. The traces, evidence and references to any identity other than Scots-Irish disappeared in my family and were buried deep, so that no one would ever remember, once those elders in the family and those in the village who knew, passed away.

What of Judah's siblings, Sarah Sharpe Barnes, Charles and Solomon Scott? Because they had darker skin, the community in which their life stories evolved was primarily that of the African-American community of the central Connecticut River Valley. In a way, for all of us descended from those four siblings, this search leads to a new perspective of ourselves as contemporary descendants of a scattered tribal people. Some of us are white Americans with Indian ancestry, some of us are black Americans with Indian ancestry. Nearly all of us have the blood of all three peoples running through our veins.

As the story of family origins unfolded, it became evident that race and racism played a defining role. As a person raised in white society in the 50s and 60s, my own experience with racism of course was always second, and third-hand. But once we began uncovering the layers of Judah's family, race and skin color became very real to me, but as a source of pride, not of shame as it had been for the last two generations of Judah's descendants.

Judah's grandfather, John Mason Strong, was labeled on the census of 1840 as a Free Person of Color. That word "free" sounded pretty good, but what did it really mean? Was he ever really free? The two names of Mason and Strong were the names of white English officers who had participated in the massacres of the Pequot and other tribal peoples in the 1600s. Yet it was apparent that our John Mason Strong, as a person of color, had no family or racial connection with these men, or did he?

Concerning the color designations recorded on the various censuses, we learned that in our family's history we were called Free People of Color, then Black, then Mulatto, then White, but not Indian. The colored Strong family, the Mason and Jeffrey families were all clearly tribal people of mixed blood oftentimes living on Indian lands. What was to be gained by listing them otherwise? Inevitably, by lifting the corner of the federal census rug, to see what was hidden there, we discovered multiple political, social, and racist objectives of the state and federal censuses.

One purpose was of course to "terminate" tribes so their lands could be made available to white farmers and investors. If there were no more tribes, then there were no more valid indigenous claims to the coveted lands. Most New England states were successful in terminating the tribes within their borders by the1880s. These terminations were patently illegal and unconstitutional since only the US Congress could do that, not the individual states. Nevertheless, it took a struggle of almost a hundred years for the Narragansett, Wampanoag, Mohegan, and Pequot to recover their status as federally recognized sovereign nations.

By the time young Judah was counted in his first census in 1860, he was listed as a mulatto. Trying to find a workable definition of that term proved challenging for us, often because of the changing meaning of the word and the subjective use of census terms.

In the Federal Census process, starting in 1790, we discovered the subjectivity of racial categories, and by extension, racist definitions, that defined and reinforced a sense of inferiority or superiority of the groups that were identified and enumerated in American society.

At the beginning of this nation, the objective of counting the citizens of the US was to determine the apportionment of representation in the House of Representatives and to determine tax responsibility. However, the census became, in fact, not a neutral affair of bean counting. For years, the census was used to categorize citizens (or three-fifths of a unit in the case of slaves) based on a subjective understanding of race, physical characteristics, and biology. Given the rise of "scientific racism" in the 1820s and 1830s, the social context in which the census was conducted made it a powerful political and economic tool, not just an enumeration instrument.

It could be very amusing to read of the efforts to define categories of citizens for the census, if the history weren't so appalling. The government's need to label, categorize, and certify its citizens in terms of racial constructs gave rise to a need to define the skin color variations, in giving instructions to the census takers. Then these people often had to consequently use their subjective understanding and judgment when they arrived at the front door. The racial designations recorded in the census then depended on who the census-taker was, and who was at home to answer the door.

At various times, we learned that census-takers used simplistic guidelines: Anglos or clearly northern Europeans were counted as White. Those of clear African origin (in the eyes of the census-taker) were listed as Black. Black slaves were counted as three fifths of a person. Mulattos could be a combination of Black and White, White and Indian, Black and Indian, or a combination of all three, hence tri-racial. Other groups called mulatto included Arabs (Moors), Jews, and Portuguese. There really weren't enough categories, not even enough room on the census sheet for all the variations, so the designation of mulatto was instituted.

Sometimes Indians were counted as Indians, but those who lived on reservations and hence were not taxable, did not get counted. Indians not on the reservation were called at times Free People of Color, mulatto, or even white. Instructions to census-takers, even in the 1790-1890 censuses, were to count quadroons, octroons, and tally the exact proportion of African blood, even to the "one drop rule". Eventually it was decided that mulattos, especially mixed white and Indian who were living in white communities should be counted as white, since they were successfully "assimilated".

So in our research of ancestors listed on the censuses, and for other searchers like us, it has proven difficult and confusing to figure out true ethnic groups based on government documents. In fact, I learned that I descended from a long line of tri-racial ancestors who were called at times Indian, Free People of Color, Black, Mulatto, Negro, White Indian, and just plain White. One of the Jeffrey ancestors in fact was listed using all of the above at different points in his lifetime!

What did that mean to Judah during his lifetime? Probably not much, since individual census information remains closed to the public for 70 years. He knew who he was, those living in his social and cultural context knew who he was, and so by self-identification, he could call himself Indian or White, and no one would necessarily seek to challenge him.

In this fearful maelstrom of labels, the contradictions and embedded dangers of being anything but white well before and after the Civil War perhaps render more understandable the desire that members of my family wished to be "assimilated".

They wished to bury deep the racial mix they carried within themselves, despite themselves.

It is clear that somewhere along the line, perhaps with Lizzie Moir Smith and her sons, there was a conscious decision to suppress and bury the story of Judah's origins, so that the sons and their descendants could be forever White.

The post Civil War racial pressure was building once again as early as the 1880s and likely became acute by the 1900s as the nation became more segregated and racist after Reconstruction. Woodrow Wilson, of Scots-Irish, hence Protestant stock like Lizzie, was certainly a racist, and he reintroduced apartheid conditions into the White House and the US government. That example more than likely both reflected and set the tone throughout the land, and certainly validated the desires of our family to become exclusively white, and to repudiate kin in the next town over.

Judah was probably a victim, knowingly or not, when near the end of his life, family pressures kept him estranged from his colored siblings living just a few miles away.

The choice of the color group with which to maintain his affiliation was forced on him by family and societal pressures.

I wonder if he actually struggled with having to deny the existence of his sister Sarah. There certainly was never a mention of her in the family, although Pete knew of one of Sarah's sons, Herbert Barnes, and knew that we were related to him, as well as to the Harris family. Somehow she had heard this, in spite of efforts to suppress the connection and the existence of the racial mix in our blood. Ironically enough, contemporary descendants of the families of Sarah, Solomon and Charles, Judah's three siblings, had never heard of *his* existence either. So the severing of family ties was complete, with neither the white side nor the black side ever mentioning the other until very recently, when we went on a search for the rest of our missing family.

Judah's son Doug was certainly a victim of the racism re-asserting itself. When the word reached the Red Sox management of Doug's mixed race, of his "having black blood", he was dropped from the lily-white team of 1912 almost overnight. The Sox were already dealing with tensions between Catholic and Protestant players, and given that certain team members were associated with the Ku Klux Klan, the management was fiercely uncompromising in their need to keep Black or Indian players out of the organization. In fact, no Black player joined the team until Pumpsie Green broke the Sox color line in the late 1960s! In Doug's case, the management let it be known in the newspapers that Doug had a "heart ailment", when in fact it was neither his heart nor his lack of talent; it was his race and extended family. Black blood was his "ailment."

That Red Sox incident was most likely the definitive crisis that drove the point clearly and cruelly home, deep into the family's heart. They closed the door on Judah's colored siblings, and the family conspiracy began. Interestingly enough in those days, of course the whole village knew of Judah, his kinfolk, and the fact that there were blacks in the family. So the knowledge of my family's origins persisted in the memories of village families, but not in mine. It seems like the whole town knew, except us. That knowledge of our colored identity persisted while the aspect of our Indian identity, which could go a long way in explaining the "colored" concept, faded from village gossip.

So where does this cycle now lead? I'm the grandson who wishes to remember. To remember, I've had to find and re-learn what was buried deep, and to try to understand, in order to pass on what should be remembered.

And what is it I choose to remember? Remember where I came from, without really knowing before? How to remember something that you never knew? How to learn about the paths taken by the ancestors, and remembering, pass it on to the ones who will come after me? Learning and then remembering, and passing it on. But what did I learn, to help explain what brought me here, what I am doing here, in this place?

I did learn about the people native to this place, not as an outsider, but as one who has discovered ancient connections to this place through them. The landscape here has always spoken to me. I've always felt effortlessly integrated into it. Coincidence, imagination or a real connection inherited from The First People who believe that they were placed here by the force they call Creator, so far back the centuries and the generations cannot be counted? I learned that many of us here still do indeed have their blood, their DNA within us, some without knowing, because those ancestors were made to be invisible.

Looking at Joseph Jeffrey's story, I learned that life in a tribe was and still is complicated, more than any outsider can grasp, even now. Joseph built the house he lived in, mastering a style that integrated and bridged the differences between Indian and English colonial. He built so well that the house is still standing 300 years later. He lost the house he built, likely due to complications of tribal politics and relentless English pressure for more land and resources. He lost it due to his association with the debt-ridden, troubled leader Tom Ninigret, and rapacious whites seeking to send the tribe into extinction. I learned that the loss of the house set in motion a chain of events, coincidences and circumstances that still echo in my own existence, that placed me here where I now live in Judah's house on the river.

I learned, and now I shall remember through the ancestors, that to survive a violent clash of cultures, to reach higher in white dominated society, many mixed blood people had to learn to become invisible, to seek to become white, whiter still, to deny kinship, to close doors tight, to deny identity, to escape the risk of being labeled as colored, which more often than not locked such colored individuals, families and peoples into a permanent status of inferiority.

I have learned that down through the ages, the generations of Jeffreys knew who they were: a tri-racial blend of Indian, European, and African. They remained people of color for the most part, although the census placed many individuals in contradictory categories every ten years: Black, Mulatto, white Indian, White, or Colored. Nevertheless, family members worked to advance people of color. They were present when colored rights needed to be defended and fought for. Amos Beman and Eunice Jeffrey were collaborators of Frederick Douglass, Nathan Jeffrey fought in the 54th Massachusetts Glory Regiment, Hester Jeffrey worked and marched alongside Susan B. Anthony, Rudolph Scott was a close friend and ally of Chief Joseph, Amos Jeffrey worked for black rights in the Life Insurance industry in 1888. These things make me proud. This is part of what I wish to remember.

I learned that part of the Joseph Jeffrey line merged with the Cooley Mason line of East Haddam, and that a child of William Mason and Rebecca Jeffrey moved up the Connecticut River to be eventually responsible for me finding myself here, generations later, still on the banks of that river.

I've re-learned that this country has almost always pre-judged and determined who you are and what you are capable of, simply by the color of your skin. We are still dealing with that. The US government, in its censuses since 1790, always made a determination that led to judgments about your character, identity, even worth and value, by putting a label on your skin color. To that point, Indians became Free People of Color, even Black, Negro, or Mulatto, but rarely Indian, so as to lead to an "extinction" of Indians, and subsequent termination of tribes by the 1880s. New England is full of "last living Indian" stories. Because we easily intermarried with blacks and whites, "real Indians" were declared extinct.

We know that right after the Civil War, there was a brief period of tolerance, acceptance, a mingling of the races. Perhaps these circumstances facilitated acceptance of Judah and his sister Sarah marrying white people within a month of each other. Great Aunt Sarah Sharpe, considered black after having been an Indian, married William Barnes, a white man, in 1881, during that period of openness. But the Ku Klux Klan and growing white hostility towards people of color put a rapid end to the interracial period.

Perhaps key to this whole story is that, at a critical point, the four siblings, Judah, Sarah, Charles, and Solomon separated, or were separated from one another as surely as if they had been sold down the river. Judah had the fortunate circumstance to be born with light skin; he had married a white woman, his label had been changed to white, and he lived as a white man in this white village. Sarah had married a white Vermont man, but nevertheless remained black, perhaps mislabeled, but black just the same for her entire life. She had six sons who were all considered black, when the designation *mulatto* was dropped. They in turn married into the black community five miles away from Judah who was also raising six sons like his sister, but they were now white.

The Scott siblings, Charles and Solomon, followed the Sarah Sharpe pattern, marrying into the black community and having descendants considered black.

What did Judah feel then in his last ten years, when he had to deny his connection and the existence of his colored siblings who were both black and Indian? Did he ever really give in to accepting the severance of his ties of kinship with Sarah, Charles, and Solomon? I'd like to think that he resisted the iron will of Lizzie, that in his heart he never denied his kin, his dual identity, his mixed blood. I'd like to think I'm remembering that for him, in his place, by telling his story. For sure, that duality ended, and the door slammed shut sometime around 1912.

That door remained shut until we discovered it 100 years later and began prying it open.

And now, having wished to stir the family memory, I have learned. I have wished to remember, I have met the ancestors, and they have given me this story. I know now that I am to be the Go-Between. Our story is not yet finished of course. And though they are from the past, they are now part of my present, continuing story. I know now how I came to be in this place.

Betsy H. Strong – David P. Brule

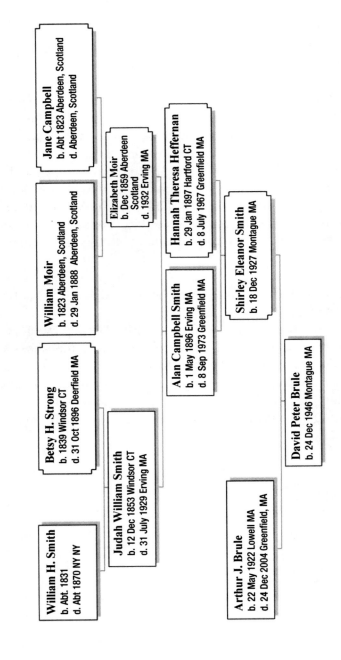

Jane Campbell
b. Abt 1823 Aberdeen, Scotland
d. Aberdeen, Scotland

William Moir
b. 1823 Aberdeen, Scotland
d. 29 Jan 1888 Aberdeen, Scotland

Elizabeth Moir
b. Dec 1859 Aberdeen Scotland
d. 1932 Erving MA

Hannah Theresa Heffernan
b. 29 Jan 1897 Hartford CT
d. 8 July 1967 Greenfield MA

Betsy H. Strong
b. 1839 Windsor CT
d. 31 Oct 1896 Deerfield MA

Alan Campbell Smith
b. 1 May 1896 Erving MA
d. 8 Sep 1973 Greenfield MA

Shirley Eleanor Smith
b. 18 Dec 1927 Montague MA

William H. Smith
b. Abt. 1831
d. Abt 1870 NY NY

Judah William Smith
b. 12 Dec 1853 Windsor CT
d. 31 July 1929 Erving MA

David Peter Brule
b. 24 Dec 1946 Montague MA

Arthur J. Brule
b. 22 May 1922 Lowell MA
d. 24 Dec 2004 Greenfield, MA

Epilogue

Back on the River 2014

"You spoke to me of the snow owl." Strong Oak said.
"You spoke of how many years you waited for him on the banks
of this river. He was meant to find you, and you, him. Sooner
or later you would see him, for he was bringing your vision, he
was your vision. He came to you when it was his time to pass
into the spirit world. You well know that when you held him
and his great talons clutched your arm, when his fierce golden
eyes looked into yours, he recognized you. He was passing his
spirit to you. He is your guide, he will help you pass between."

The snow is fresh-falling in the late afternoon of a dark
January. It's the right time to take this walk far out on the point
under the towering pines. Snow filters down through needles
on the sweeping branches. Pale light and graceful whiteness
transform the landscape. Here, the two worlds are very close to
one another.

Far out on the sheltered cove, a fire blazes orange near the
cluster of men and boys fishing through the ice. Twenty feet
below them, under that ice of the sunken, flooded meadow, lie
10,000 years of hearth fires and village sites where the first
River People lived.

The fishermen don't see me, invisible on my solitary walk
at the end of this story, at the end of this journey.

I step out from the pine woods on the long rocky point
that leads to the edge of the split in the rock where the
Connecticut still moves as it has for millennia, and in spite of
this year's January ice. This bedrock arm once stretched across
to the other shore, forming a barrier here thousands of years
ago. The red rock ridge unyielding, the river had to flow over

this natural dam, creating three waterfalls. The top edge of the barrier where the waters cascaded is now dry and exposed, sharp-edged still, and pine-fringed. The isolated plunge pools below are now frozen over and silent.

Out at the farthest tip of this rocky reach, the river finally forced its passage through one of the waterfalls at the place we call the Narrows, the gap where 10,000 years ago, the water split the rock.

In the gathering dusk, I can look down on the sullen current of the now placid river; here and there swirls rise up from unknown depths. The waterfall that finally wore out the rock flows mysteriously upward from deep below.

From here, below me, I can see the watery pathway I took in those days back 60 years ago, when as a young boy I drifted through the gap in the fog with my constant dog-- when we were all young, and this story was unknown to me, perhaps just forming. The boy who passed over these dark ancient waters just there below, could he not have looked up to the rocky bluff and spy himself now nearing 70 years of age, peering down, this dark January afternoon? And finally it feels I've come full circle.

I come here to ponder, now and again, when I feel the need to get back in touch with the flow of time. Much of my life has played out in this landscape, within a radius of barely more than a mile.

Looking across the Narrows, I can make out my childhood home, a light from my mother and father's house still faint in the dusk above. A mile beyond lies the hospital where I was born, the schools I attended. My father toiled for 40 years just over there, within sight of this river flowing by its islands. My grandparents, now dead and gone and buried in the cemetery just over yonder, had homes just a short distance from here. Their ancestors, and therefore mine, came from river people going far back and away to the earliest tribes living along the Connecticut. I've learned that I'm deeply rooted and integrated into this riverscape of the ancient valley. Here I feel at home.

In spite of the wanderlust of my early years, I came back to live out my life within a mile from where I was born. I have come to understand that I came back to stay because there would be a story that would be revealed to me and that I was meant to tell it. Those people who put me here, the *métis* from Québec, the Celts, the Africans, the Tribal People, have blended in me. They all provided me with this story, now mostly told. I want to remember and to claim them all.

Time to drift back homewards, at the end of this winter day. I am often prone to think thoughts like these nowadays. Maybe they should be kept between myself and that gray barred owl who has been watching me.

Slightly ruffled by my musings and maybe the chill, he peers at me through eyes of liquid obsidian. Politely, I move in a wide arc away from his perch in the hemlock, leaving him to his winter's night of hunting. Thinking I can't see him, he queries with his *who-who*, leaving me to wonder even more. *Who* indeed am I? What more is there to be revealed? Am I red, white, and black all at the same time? Am I really the One Who Goes Between? And does it really matter?

I stop at my spirit tree, an ironwood, growing here for as long as I can remember. This tree is aged, grey, sinuous, and almost invisible. Its trunk is small in girth, but muscular and stubborn. It carries its name of ironwood well. I like to grapple a bit with this survivor. I push and pull against its rock-hard strength, testing my sinew against its unyielding force. Can't budge it. Don't want to anyway. Just testing our mutual endurance, to wrestle a bit, to draw into myself some of this tree's perseverance.

Back on the path home, old voices fill my head. Bits of conversation, ancestors conversing, chanting in many tongues. This place is alive with spirits, some are echoes of restless murmurings and mourning, others sing songs of happiness, of immortality, trying out their new shapes and their voices again.

The knowing owl calls from behind me softly, keeping his winter's evening, and interrogating the fading light.

Works That Have Served as Sources of Information and Inspiration

Bruchac, Hart, Wobst ,eds. *Indigenous Archaeologies*. Walnut Creek, California: Left Coast Press, Inc. 2010

Mandell, Daniel R. *Tribe, Race, History. Native Americans in Southern New England. 1780-1880.* Baltimore: Johns Hopkins University Press, 2007

Nerburn, Kent. *Neither Wolf Nor Dog. On Forgotten Roads With An Indian Elder*. Novato, California: New World Library, 1994

Nowlin, Bill,ed. *Opening Fenway Park In Style The 1912 World Champion Red Sox.* Phoenix:SABR Digital Library, 2012

Rose, James, and Brown, Barbara. *Tapestry: A Living History of the Black Family in Southeastern Connecticut.* New London: New London County Historical Society, 1979

Savage, Kelly. *The Pond Dwellers: the People of the Freshwaters of Massachusetts 1620-1676.* Wales, MA: Panther Publishing, 1996

Simmons and Simmons, eds. *Old Light on Separate Ways: the Narragansett Diary of Joseph Fish.* Hanover and London: University Press of New   England, 1982

Smith, Mrs. Jane T.(Hills). *The Last of the Nehantics* Niantic, CT: East Lyme Library Publishing, 2011

Tayac, Gabrielle, ed. *Indivisible: African-Native American Lives in the Americas*. Washington: Smithsonian Institution's National Museum of the American Indian, 2009

Welch, Vicki S. *And They Were Related Too: A Study of Eleven Generations of One American Family!* Xlibris Corporation, 2006

CPSIA information can be obtained at www.ICGtesting.com
Printed in the USA
BVOW04s0425100415

395605BV00006B/20/P

9 781634 901260